THE TIN BOX

A SAMMY & BRIAN MYSTERY #9

BY KEN MUNRO

GASLIGHT PUBLISHERS

The Tin Box

Gaslight Publishers
P. O. Box 258
Bird-in-Hand, PA 17505

E-mail: sammybrian@desupernet.net

Library of Congress Number: 99-70700
International Standard Book Number: 1-883294-84-3

Printed 1999 by
Masthof Press
220 Mill Road
Morgantown, PA 19543-9701

DEDICATION

*This book is for
all the parents and educators
who encourage children to read.*

*Special thanks to:
Michael Baksa
Det. Sgt. E. J. Abel
Sandy Weidel
and Michelle Baker*

CHAPTER ONE

T he crack that rimmed the stone caused Brian's wildest dream to burst into reality. Ever since his best friend, Sammy Wilson, had moved into the old house, Brian had fantasized about finding buried treasure within its walls. The young amateur detective had no doubts. Any two-hundred-year-old house with a stone wall cellar had to be hiding some secrets.

It was while Sammy and Brian, Bird-in-Hand's fifteen-year-old amateur detectives, were working on their science fair projects that Brian was distracted to a better cause. The stone that protruded from the cellar wall had a sliver of a slit surrounding it. Helm, Brian Helm, otherwise known (to himself) as double-oh-seven and a half, had to investigate.

Brian Helm, secret agent, placed his hands on the stone. Did he dare to remove the stone? Would moving the stone cause the wall to open, exposing a hidden room? Would its slightest movement cause the walls and ceiling to come crashing down? He glanced over at his "chief" busy in the corner of the cellar. Would extracting the stone be putting both their lives in danger? His frown slipped into a smile. When you're double-oh-seven and a half, danger is your middle name.

Brian nudged the stone back and forth. It moved slightly. He wiggled it, pulling it toward him. It was like pulling a large, loose tooth. The stone moaned and resisted as Brian tugged it forward. It wasn't about to give up its place in history—not without a struggle.

The air of anticipation that surrounded Brian's quest for any prize that might lie behind the stone was disturbed by his friend's voice. "Brian, we came down here to work on our science fair projects, not for you to dismantle my house."

"But the stone's loose. That means someone had it out before," said Brian, without releasing his grip on the stone.

Sammy walked over to see how much damage Brian had done to the wall. He also needed to give his friend a reason for any cracks there. Sammy was tall and slim with straight dark hair and serious blue eyes. Brian was short with wavy brown hair and devilish hazel eyes.

"Brian, this house has shifted and settled in the last two hundred years, causing the cracks."

Brian let his arms drop as he turned toward Sammy. He arched his eyebrows and raised his hands, palms up. "Okay, but I'm telling you, there's something hidden behind that stone. You know George Washington traveled through Bird-in-Hand years and years ago."

"So?" asked Sammy.

"So, there could be a letter written by him right there behind that stone."

Sammy shook his head. "Brian, I don't think George Washington used that wall as a mailbox."

"Well, you know what I mean," said Brian. He turned and tapped his finger on the stone. "George's secret plans could be hidden right here, right now." He threw his hands into the air in a dramatic fashion. "But, okay, if you want to miss out on the find of the century, I'll just push this stone back against old George's historic plans for the Battle of Gettysburg."

"You mean his plans for the Revolutionary War. The battle at Gettysburg was during the Civil War," said Sammy.

Brian's face lit up. "Oh, then you mean George Washington's letter that is behind this stone tells of his Revolutionary War plans." Brian's hands again gripped the stone. "Then we better remove the stone and release the letter from its prison." He hesitated and looked at Sammy for final approval.

Realizing he was influenced by his partner's words, Sammy smiled and nodded. "Go ahead, pull it out. Just don't be disappointed when you find only dirt behind the stone." He darted around Brian's science project to give a hand.

Brian didn't need help. With renewed energy, he wiggled and pulled at the stone. Without warning it plopped from the wall, sending Brian bouncing off Sammy. Regaining his balance, Brian stooped and laid the stone on the floor. He quickly stood and faced the hole that led to the past.

"Well?" asked Sammy. "Anything there?"

Brian didn't know if his mind was playing tricks on him or if he did see an object back in the darkened hole. "I see something," he said. "I see something."

Brian's hand trembled as it tunneled deeper into the dirt hole. He extended his fingers as if he expected to shake hands with Thomas Jefferson or Thomas Edison. His fingernails scraped against metal. He reached in further, pawing at whatever was there and clamped his fingers around the object and pulled it from the hole.

It was a tin box!

While Sammy was greatly surprised at Brian's find, he wasn't about to be caught up in a reckless frenzy. His experience as an amateur detective had taught him to put reason before emotion. "Brian, give me the box. We don't want to destroy any evidence."

"It's not evidence," yelled Brian. "It's gold— a box of gold!"

"Whatever happened to Washington's secret battle plans?" asked Sammy.

"Well, okay—George threw in some gold coins to save for after the battle. Oh, I don't know. Come on. Open it," said Brian, reluctantly passing the box to Sammy.

The young detective handled the box as though it was a moon rock. He inspected it closely. The four-by-six-inch box was one inch deep. Corrosion and rust had distorted some of the printing that had once advertised its contents. "It's an old Hershey Chocolate tin."

Brian held on to some hope. "But Hershey is a very old chocolate company. Right, Sammy?"

"Yes, over a hundred years," he said, studying what remained of the address. "But I'm sorry, old pal, this tin box is no more than thirty-five years old."

"Thirty-five? How do you know that?"

Sammy turned the end of the box for Brian to see. "The address has a zip code. The post office developed zip codes in the early sixties."

"Oh," said Brian, grimacing. Any hope of a major find was disappearing quickly.

"Look here," continued Sammy. "The lid is sealed with wax. It means someone wanted to protect its contents from the elements."

A smile returned to Brian's face. "So it contains something valuable," he said. "Open it. Open it."

Sammy shook the box gently. An object inside slid against something that deadened the sound. "This could be someone's attempt at a time capsule. Maybe we should put it back."

"Put it back. You're crazy," said Brian. "I know you. You couldn't sleep at night if—" Brian saw the small smile that crept across Sammy's face. "You're kidding. Right, Sammy?"

Sammy picked up the knife from the card table supporting Brian's science project. He slid the tip of the blade through the wax that sealed the lid. He then guided the knife around the edge until the seal was broken.

"Hurry up. Open it," said Brian, moving in closer. He didn't want to miss a thing.

The lid came off easier than Sammy had thought. He quickly set the knife and lid on the table and returned his attention to the contents of the tin box.

He saw two items inside.

"You were right, Brian," said Sammy. "There is gold in here."

Brian smiled. "Really?" He put his hand on Sammy's arm to lower the box. Then he, too, saw the gold.

A gold pocket watch.

As Brian snatched up the watch for a closer look, Sammy carefully unfolded what appeared to be a newspaper article. His arm swept aside pieces of his friend's project, clearing enough area to support the article. His eye caught the date at the top. January 20, 1977.

While Sammy read the news item, Brian examined the pocket watch. It was old. He wondered if watches existed back in George

Washington's time. Maybe George timed himself as he crossed the Delaware. Brian remembered the painting he had seen in his history book. Did Washington's hand hold a watch as he stood in the boat? Brian's bubble burst when he read the inscription on the back. "To Charles Farrell for twenty-five years of service." The date September 7, 1943, was stamped below. Visions of reporters and photographers pushing and shoving to interview Sammy and him as they held the tin box, faded quickly. He pressed the watch stem and the cover sprang open, displaying the hands fixed at 3:10.

"It's just a dumb, old pocket watch," said Brian, snapping the cover closed. "It has writing on the back." He held the watch up in Sammy's direction and made a sour face. "I hope I get more than a dumb watch after I work for twenty-five years."

"Why? What does it say?" asked Sammy, glancing up from his reading.

"To Charles Farrell for twenty-five years of service."

Sammy's face turned white.

CHAPTER TWO

"W hat's wrong?" asked Brian. In all the years he had known Sammy, he had never seen such a look.

Finally Sammy broke the stare and returned his attention to the news item. "This article is from the Lancaster newspaper dated 1977. It's about Shawn Walker, a nineteen-year-old college student in Greensboro, North Carolina, who went for a hike during his college break." Sammy paused and looked at Brian. "Shawn Walker never returned from the trip. His abandoned car was found parked near the trail. The police suspected foul play."

"So?" asked Brian.

"The police and some experienced hikers and climbers searched the mountain trail for a week and never found him, dead or alive. His parents hired an investigator to continue the search. He, too, found nothing. Their son had just vanished."

"I don't get it," said Brian. "Why the strange look on your face?"

"One theory the police had," continued Sammy, "was that Walker fell, hit his head, and developed amnesia." He looked down at the article and used his finger as a guide. "Now comes the interesting part." Sammy read directly from the paper. "Should you come in contact with anyone who is disoriented and has symptoms of amnesia, check for this one item. His parents said their son was never without it. It was his grandfather's gold pocket watch given to him after his grandfather died. Inscribed on the back were the words, To Charles Farrell for twenty-five years of service."

"Wow!" said Brian as he glanced at the watch to confirm that the words were the same. "This is the watch! This is the watch!"

Sammy took the watch from Brian and frowned. He didn't say anything to his friend for it was too late. Brian's fingerprints would be all over the watch. Except— He pushed the stem and the cover snapped open. A glass crystal protected the face of the watch. "Brian, did you touch any part of this glass?"

Brian was already wondering how the pocket watch traveled from Greensboro, North Carolina, to Bird-in-Hand, Pennsylvania. "No. No, I don't think so."

Holding the watch by its stem, Sammy now considered the timepiece as evidence. Evidence in what, he wasn't sure. He did know he would have to turn the tin box and its contents over to the police.

"Does the paper have a picture of this guy?" asked Brian.

"Yeah, but it's yellow and faded like the rest of the article."

Brian moved closer and glanced down. "He looks like a hippy, all that long hair."

"That's how he looked twenty-two years ago," said Sammy. "No telling how he would look today— if he's still alive."

Brian snickered.

"Now what?" asked Sammy.

"I was just thinking," said Brian. "Even if he's dead, he wouldn't look the same."

"You're weird, Brian. Do you know that? You're weird."

"Weird but lovable," replied Brian. "Hey, if Shawn Walker is alive, what was he doing here— in this house?"

"Maybe he wasn't," said Sammy. "Maybe someone else brought the watch to Bird-in-Hand. He headed for the steps. "Come on. Leave everything as it is. We need to call our friend, Detective Ben Phillips. Let the police handle it from here."

Brian raised his finger and spoke to Sammy's back. "Hey, remember I found the box. It was my uncanny ability to snoop out hidden stuff that found that watch. And . . . and . . . so when Channel 8 interviews us—"

The cellar was pitched into darkness as Sammy reached the top step and turned off the light.

"Hey, it's dark down here!" yelled Brian. "Put the light back on so I can see!"

"Why don't you use your uncanny ability to find your way past all the other 'stuff' that's down there. Like dead bodies and snakes and—"

"Yipes!" screamed Brian as vivid images propelled him, stumbling up the stairs past his friend.

Sammy turned and faced Brian who was already standing by the open door to the kitchen. "Should I also tell Channel 8 that you're afraid of the dark?"

"I wasn't afraid," said Brian. "I just rushed up so I could hold the door open for my buddy who would never say anything bad about me." Brian then produced his broad mechanical smile, bowed, and motioned for Sammy to enter the kitchen.

Sammy shook his head and went for the phone.

Photographs were taken of the cellar, the wall, the stone, and the tin box with its contents. After the Record and Identification officers finished dusting for prints, they returned to the station. Detective Phillips remained behind. He closed the lid and slipped the tin box into an evidence bag. He took one last look around and followed the teen-age, amateur detectives upstairs to Sammy's room.

The old house went into shock as Phillips' two-hundred-twenty-two-pound, six-foot-two frame hustled up the stairs and into the bedroom. His bulk and piercing eyes reached out from above a thin mustache. They compelled many criminals to confess their sins.

These same eyes, however, looked kindly upon Sammy and Brian. Having no sons of his own, Detective Phillips considered the boys his adopted sons. They made his job easier with their crime-solving ability. Several of his cases were now closed as a result of their super sleuthing. Their insights and natural instincts for seeing the obvious brought the guilty to justice.

Newspaper accounts of the boys' exploits showed Detective Ben Phillips heavily involved in their pursuits. Sometimes he assisted the boys, and sometimes they assisted him. He supplied the muscle and authority; they supplied the innocence and curiosity of youth.

Brian hurried into his position on the bed before Phillips claimed it. With Sammy settled in behind his oak desk, the only seat remaining was the rocking chair—the chair Joyce Myers used when she helped the boys with some of their cases.

The you-can't-be-serious look on the boys' faces as Phillips headed for the small rocker was not missed by the detective. He stopped and analyzed the situation. The horrified expression etched in the folds of the rocker's cushions was reason enough for Phillips to stop and plop down on the floor beside the desk. He placed the evidence bag beside him. "I better sit here. I wouldn't want to put that old rocker out of its misery."

"The rocking chair and Joyce Myers thanks you," said Sammy.

Phillips smiled. "I guess you boys have this case practically solved by now. Well, what do you think?"

"The watch was brought here by either Shawn Walker or someone else," said Sammy. "If it was someone else, he could be a murderer, a kidnapper, or a thief. Which makes me wonder if his parents got a ransom demand after their son disappeared."

"I think it was murder," said Brian to the ceiling. "Serial killers collect things from their victims. Right, Sammy?"

"But the items in the box belong to only one person," said Sammy.

"Maybe Shawn Walker was the serial killer's first victim."

Sammy rolled his eyes and leaned back in his chair, placing his hands behind his head. "I was thinking. This happened twenty-two years ago. Maybe Shawn Walker is back home by now."

"That's a thought," said Phillips. He checked his watch. "Let's see. It's 11:05, Saturday morning. When I get back to the station, I'm going to call the Greensboro police and tell them what we found. If the case is closed or still open, they can bring us up-to-date with whatever information they have."

"If he was back home, wouldn't he have the watch?" asked Brian. "Remember the newspaper said he was never without the watch."

"It appears someone parted him from his watch," said Sammy.

"Well, whatever," said Phillips. "The date on the paper was 1977. That's twenty-two years ago. The first thing we should check is the person who owned this house at that time."

"After I called you, I told my parents about what we found in—"

"What *I* found," corrected Brian.

"What *you* found in the cellar, and they said Alice and Albert Mellinger owned the house in 1977." Sammy waved his thumb. "They now live on Beechdale Road."

Detective Phillips grabbed the evidence bag and stood. "Let me take this bag to the station. I'll place a call to the Greensboro police, tell them about the box, and see what I can find out about Shawn Walker." He took a deep breath. "It's going to be a long day."

"You won't forget about us. Will you?" asked Sammy.

"I'll do a background check on the Mellingers and then pay them a visit. I could pick you boys up in about two hours if you're interested in going along."

Brian did a quick sit-up on the bed. "Hey, are you kidding?"

Sammy smiled and nodded. He was pleased that Phillips included them in this investigation.

He realized Detective Phillips was being practical. He needed all the help he could get to solve a twenty-two-year-old mystery.

"I know the Mellingers," said Sammy. "I'd hate to think of them as suspects."

"Really?" said Phillips, heading for the door. "Well, then think of them as murderers."

CHAPTER THREE

O n the drive over to interview the Mellingers, Detective Ben Phillips told the boys that he had phoned the Greensboro police. Their records showed that Shawn Walker was still missing and presumed dead. However, because of the discovered pocket watch, they would be sending a detective to Lancaster.

Something terrible *had* happened to Shawn Walker. It would now be up to Ben Phillips, Sammy Wilson, and Brian Helm to continue the investigation.

The Mellingers lived in a small ranch house on Beechdale Road, several miles back from Main Street. Detective Phillips had phoned the Mellingers to make arrangements for the interview. However, he did not tell them about the tin box.

The late October chilly air had already whispered its message to the trees. Colored leaves cloaked the ground, waiting for winter's arrival.

Phillips's suit coat was enough to ward off the chill. The boys wore sweaters.

It was no surprise to Phillips and the teen-age detectives to be greeted at the door by two nervous senior citizens in their sixties. Albert and Alice quickly ushered their company into a very neat and cozy living room.

Brian spied a green candy jar with a lid. When Sammy and Phillips were directed to overstuffed chairs, Brian selected a chair near the window—next to the table that held the candy.

When everyone got comfortable, they waited for Detective Phillips to speak. But he said nothing. Instead he gazed at the opened folder he held in his hand.

Sammy recognized the interrogating technique Phillips was using. An unexpected silence provided time for the suspect to ponder his wrongdoings. The opened folder also created the impression that the police knew more than they did. Sometimes it was what the police didn't say that could make a felon confess.

"I guess you know why we're here," said Phillips when he felt the Mellingers were primed and ready to relieve themselves of any guilt they harbored.

"No, no, we don't," said Alice Mellinger. "We pay our taxes." Her hand quivered as she brushed it back over her graying hair that was properly twisted into a bun. Her hand returned to her lap where it joined the other hand in toying with the folds in her flannel dress. Her light gray eyes met Phillips's unflinching gaze then turned to her husband, expecting him to disarm the threat that filled the room.

Brian's hazel eyes gazed again at the candy jar. Could he lift the lid and free some of the captive jellybeans without making a sound?

Albert Mellinger appeared willing to wait out the plan of attack initiated by the detective. His head rested back on the recliner that faced the television. That was his chair, his domain. Alfred was sixty-five, several years older than his wife. While she had remained slim, he had put on weight. He was also aware of the bald spot developing toward the back of his head. The coldness of the recliner's leather pinpointed the area. Alfred had been a business man before he retired. His cautious attitude showed that he could still converse with the best of them, even in a reclining position. Though unsure of the situation, he smiled. "We don't have a clue as to why you're here," he finally said.

"You lived on Main Street twenty-two years ago in the house now occupied by Sammy Wilson and his parents."

"Yes, we know the Wilsons," said Alfred. "They have the Bird-in-Hand Country Store. We sold the house ten years ago to Mr. Dexter who then recently sold the house to the Wilsons."

"Sammy and Brian found a tin box that was hidden about twenty-two years ago. It was hidden in the house at the time you lived there," proclaimed Phillips in a commanding voice.

Three sets of eyes darted back and forth between Alice and Alfred Mellinger.

"What tin box?" asked Alice, her voice reflecting the confusion in her eyes.

"The one containing the gold watch belonging to a Mr. Shawn Walker from Greensboro, North Carolina," answered Phillips.

Sammy watched as the Mellingers glanced at each other. They seemed genuinely surprised at the mention of a tin box, a gold watch, and a person called Shawn Walker. Had they prepared themselves for any questions the police might ask? wondered Sammy. Were they capable twenty years ago of harming a nineteen-year-old college student? Were the Mellingers concealing a secret? Sammy didn't expect the Mellingers to confess to murder, but he did expect them to admit knowing about the tin box.

"I didn't hide a tin box. Did you, Alice?" asked Alfred.

"No," she replied quickly.

"How do you know the box was hidden twenty-two years ago?" asked Alfred.

"The date on the news article found inside was 1977 and also because of the corroded condition of the box," said Phillips.

Because of Phillips' strong voice and interest in his explanation, the soft thud behind them went unnoticed. Brian had lifted the glass lid—slowly and carefully. In his attempt not to draw attention to himself, his hand flinched and tipped the jar. Its contents landed on the carpeted floor.

Phillips continued the interrogation. "Have you two ever been in Greensboro, North Carolina?"

The look that passed between the Mellingers was loaded with guilt and was not missed by Phillips or Sammy.

Alfred sat forward on the recliner. "We have a daughter and son-in-law who live in Gainesville, Florida. We pass through North Carolina on the way down, but we never stop there. And we've never been to Greensboro," he added.

"Did you visit your daughter in January of 1977?" asked the detective.

Alice stood and went over to the fireplace. "Yes, we did," she said as she picked up a framed photograph from the mantel.

Her quick, firm answer surprised Phillips. "How can you be certain you were there January 1977?"

"We go to Gainesville every year," she said to the picture. "We leave in January right after the holidays and return at the end of the month." She turned and held the photograph for them to see. "This is our daughter, her husband, and their two children," she said proudly.

"So you pass through North Carolina twice every January. Is that correct?" stated the detective, making notes inside the folder.

"That's right," said Alice, replacing the picture on the mantel. She glanced back at Brian. It was his rigid configuration that caught her attention.

The candy jar and its contents sat proudly next to Brian. An awkward smile was plastered on his face. His elbows rested on the arms of the chair, his hands stuck up in the air. His bent fingers were separated in a claw-like fashion, leaving his sticky and multicolored fingers exposed.

Alice joined her husband at the recliner. With a look of concern, she bent toward Sammy and whispered, "Tell me, does your friend have a medical condition?"

Everyone looked back at Brian.

At first, Sammy was surprised at the coloration on Brian's hands. But then he observed the candy jar with its lid slightly tipped and two jellybeans on the carpet under the table.

Sammy coughed, got their attention, and winked. "Yes, I'm afraid Brian does have a medical condition. It's called candyitus. Brian doesn't like me talking about his affliction, but I'm really not the one *spilling the beans*."

A chuckle was joined with several grins.

Brian, not one to miss a chance to perform, and needing a chance to cover his embarrassment, stood and smiled. "I learned something here today. There are sixty-six jellybeans in that jar."

Alfred looked up at his wife, reached for her

hand, and then focused back on Phillips. He shrugged. "What's the big deal about the box, the watch, and this Walker from North Carolina?" he asked, wanting to get this intrusion into his life over and done with.

Phillips closed the folder and ran his finger and thumb along his thin mustache. "We're not sure at this point. It may be nothing. We thought you might know something about the box that was found. That's all." Phillips stood to leave.

Alfred let out a sigh of relief and wiggled out of the recliner. Eager for the ominous company to leave, Alfred extended his hand. "I'm sorry we couldn't help you."

Phillips shook his hand, and thanked Alice and him for their time.

As an afterthought, Alfred said unexpectedly, "You know, we weren't the only ones living in that house in 1977."

The interview that seemed destined to go nowhere just opened up to new possibilities.

Phillips reclaimed his chair and sat. "Go on."

Alfred remained standing. "We had two boarders with us at the time."

"Ah," said Phillips, opening his folder.

"Our daughter got married and moved away," said Alice. "We were alone and needed the extra money, with the cost of the wedding and all."

"Did the boarders have access to the whole house?" asked the detective.

"Pretty much," said Alice.

"Even the cellar and attic?" asked Sammy.

"We allowed them to store their extra belongings there."

Phillips added more notes to the folder, then asked, "And their names?"

"Oh, my," sighed Alfred. "That was over twenty years ago. We had quite a few people in and out over the years."

"Ray Miller, a thin young man, was one," said Alice Mellinger. "Moore was another one. Oh, Alfred, what was his first name?" asked Alice.

"Dennis," replied her husband. "Dennis Moore, and he still owes us a month's rent."

"Remember Nancy?" asked Alice, pleased with herself as to how easy the names and memories were coming back. "I wonder what she's doing now?" she continued.

Alfred smiled. "She's the one who was a waitress at the Bird-in-Hand Family Restaurant."

Sammy and Brian listened as the Mellingers reminisced and Phillips recorded the names and information.

After the Mellingers told them everything they could remember about each of the five boarders, Phillips and the boys thanked them again and left.

In the car driving back to Sammy's house, Phillips said, "Brian, please don't touch the upholstery with your sticky hands."

Brian lifted his hands that showed faint signs of color. "It's okay, I licked them." He crossed his hands over his chest. "It has to be one of the boarders. Right, Sammy?"

"It's going to be hard tracking down those people after all these years," added Sammy.

Brian leaned over from the back seat. "Twenty-two years. That's seven years before we were born."

"I'll see what I can come up with," said Phillips. "I didn't recognize any of the names. Did you boys?"

Both boys shook their heads.

"What did you think about the Mellingers?" asked Brian.

"I checked into their background. It's clean," said Phillips. "But my feelings are that Alfred was hiding something." He peered at Sammy and Brian through the rearview mirror. "But then, we all have something to hide. Don't we?" The mirror only helped to intensify the piercing effect of his dark eyes.

Brian's subconscious mind suddenly shot forth all his misdeeds. A list, Brian was sure Phillips could see and read at that very moment. If only he could take his guilt, seal it in a tin box, and make it disappear forever.

The one element in their life that the super sleuths could not make go away was the media. The newspaper and television reporters were waiting for the boys as Phillips dropped them off in front of the house and sped away. The news of the tin box had spread quickly.

Brian stood tall and smiled as he faced the reporters. "Don't forget to tell them that I found the box," he whispered to his friend.

Sammy leaned close to Brian's ear. "There are some things I won't have to tell them. They can see for themselves."

"What's that?" whispered Brian.

"Your hair is a mess. Your face is dirty. And you have something coming out your nose."

"Huh?" said Brian, his hands flailing about.

Too late. They were being photographed and bombarded with questions. The pictures later would show Brian with a horrible expression on his face and Sammy sporting a large grin.

CHAPTER FOUR

A normal amount of excitement was shown when Sammy and Brian arrived at school on Monday. Their classmates and teachers at Conestoga Valley High School downplayed the celebrity status the boys had earned over the years. As far as the school and the community were concerned, the boys were regular guys. Sammy would have it no other way. However, Brian, who thrived on the attention, always had his pen ready to sign autographs.

It was during their third period class that Sammy and Brian were summoned to the office. As they stood in front of the receptionist, Vicky Weiler, they heard whistling coming from the principal's office. There was no mistaking the tune, "Whistle While You Work."

"Gee, Mr. Baksa must be in a good mood," said Brian, who smiled for the first time since being told that the principal wanted to see them at the office.

Vicky smiled. "He's always whistling around here. Wait until you hear his rendition of 'London Bridge Is Falling Down.'" She motioned toward the opened door. "You can go in now."

The office was spacious, containing a large desk and a round table. Cushioned chairs provided ample seating. Two hanging plants decorated the window. A poster of Chicago and a framed diploma claimed the wall behind the desk. The principal looked up and smiled.

Mike Baksa was in his early forties, wore glasses, and combed his brown hair straight back. He was tall, husky and usually sported a smile that projected his positive attitude. He nodded. "Sit down. I have a favor to ask of you." He leaned forward with his elbows on the desk and waited as Sammy and Brian selected two chairs.

Brian rubbed his hands over the wooden arms. Why couldn't Detective Phillips have an office and chairs like this? he wondered. He visualized Phillips's cramped space with its two folding metal chairs. Sammy appreciated the spacious office. There was room for thinking without feeling closed in. He adjusted his chair and then noticed the day-old newspaper lying on the desk.

Mr. Baksa snapped the paper. "Congratulations. I read here in the *Sunday News* about your discovery. Even saw you on television." He pointed to Brian. "And, Brian, you should smile more."

Brian frowned. "Yeah, well, Sammy told me . . ." He let the thought die.

"You really put Lancaster County and Conestoga Valley High School on the map again," said Baksa. "It's exciting to have you boys as students because of the good things you bring to CV." Mr. Baksa leaned back in his chair. "You have generated a lot of interest in your exploits as amateur detectives. You make excellent role models for the younger children." He paused. "Would you two boys be interested in talking to our elementary school students about some of your cases? Especially about finding the tin box and what the contents suggest."

"Yes, we would," said Sammy. He didn't have to consult his friend, Brian, who was always willing to talk—about himself.

"What I would like to do," said the principal, "is to set up a time for you to be excused from class, and then I would drive you to the elementary school and bring you back."

"That's great," said Brian. He liked the idea of getting out of class and performing in front of younger children.

"How much time will we have to talk?" asked Sammy.

"I think an hour should do it," said the principal. "The children will want to ask questions."

Brian was all smiles. "Sure, we can talk for more than an hour if you want. Right, Sammy?"

"An hour will be fine," said Mr. Baksa. He glanced at the newspaper and leaned closer to the boys. "I'm curious. What were you doing in the cellar?"

"We were working on our science fair projects," said Sammy.

"Ah," said the principal. "Are you going to win first prize again this year?"

"I don't think about that," replied Sammy. "I just want to work through a challenging problem."

Mr. Baksa stood. "Well said. Okay, you can return to your class. Look, if I can arrange it, will tomorrow be too soon for your visit to an elementary class?"

"No, that's okay," said Sammy as he headed for the door.

Brian followed. "Hey, the kids will want to hear my life's story."

Sammy let out a sigh. This was going to be tougher than he thought.

———————◆———————

After Sammy arrived home, he received a phone message from Detective Phillips. If available, the boys were to meet him at the police station. A new development had arisen in the case.

Fifteen minutes later the young detectives propped their bicycles against the building and entered the police station. Sammy expected to be directed to Phillips' office, but instead, Brian and he were taken to the conference room.

The medium-sized room was plain, no windows. Six people sat around a large oak table.

Some were drinking coffee from plastic cups. All heads turned when Sammy and Brian entered the room.

" . . . and these are the boys we've been waiting for—Sammy Wilson and Brian Helm," said Phillips as he stood and introduced the teens. "You made more than a tin box appear. The media has spread the news about your find, and these five people from Greensboro, North Carolina, showed up. They're all interested in Shawn Walker."

Brian looked at "The North Carolina Five." He stood tall and threw his shoulders back. Wow, he thought to himself, and all because I took a stone from a wall.

Sammy glanced at the four men and the woman and wondered what connection each had to the missing teenager. He took a pen and notebook from his pocket.

Ben Phillips pointed. "Boys, that is Les Gray. He was a close friend of Shawn Walker."

The man squirmed and coughed. Finally he stood and nodded. He was tall and thin, forty-two, and had wavy, red hair. "I'm the only one who can identify Shawn," he said. "I knew him better than anyone, even his own parents." He sat and continued to look uncomfortable in his new surroundings.

"Next is Art Hansen, a writer. He's writing a story about the missing Shawn Walker."

Mr. Hansen stood. He was in his sixties, short, with a medium build. He wore wire-rimmed glasses and had graying hair. He spoke softly. "I was a newspaper reporter when Walker disappeared. I'm thinking of doing a book now that his watch has been found. I'd like to interview you later if I could."

"Sure, anytime," said Brian in a deep voice, projecting his secret agent attitude.

"And this is Detective Ann Flowers from the Greensboro, North Carolina, Police Department. She's going to spend a couple of days here, helping with the investigation."

Detective Flowers didn't bother to stand or to smile. "Hi," was all she managed to say. She was thirty-three, five seven, husky, her blond hair pulled into a ponytail. Her blue pant suit was unwrinkled. She was a seasoned detective and all business.

"Do you want to introduce your friend?" asked Phillips, nodding toward the man sitting next to the female detective.

The man stood as Ann Flowers said, "This is Leon Bradley. This was his case twenty-two years ago. He's retired from the force but wanted to accompany me on this trip."

Leon Bradley was fifty-five. He was short, slim, and bald and had a strong commanding voice. "I'm here in an unofficial capacity. I won't consider myself completely retired until this case is resolved." His words echoed off the walls.

"Our last visitor from Greensboro is . . ." Detective Phillips consulted his notes. " . . . is Dirk

Evans, a private detective and executive director of The Evans Missing Persons Foundation. Its business is to investigate and find missing individuals. The project was created by Dr. Fred Walker a year after his son disappeared. It's now supported by the interest earned from the trust fund set up for Shawn Walker after the doctor died."

Dirk Evans stood and shook hands with the boys. The private investigator was of medium height and muscular. At fifty-nine years of age, he had a full head of salt and pepper hair. A large nose was his prominent feature. "I was in the security business when Dr. Walker hired me to find his son. The missing persons venture grew as a result of that. I promised Doctor Walker that I would find his son. After he died, he left his entire estate, two million dollars, to Shawn. As Detective Phillips just said, the money is in a trust fund, waiting for Shawn to return and claim it."

"I wonder if Shawn Walker knows he has two million dollars waiting for him back in North Carolina?" asked Sammy.

"Not if he's dead," said Detective Ann Flowers, short and to the point. She wanted the meeting to end so she could make a phone call.

Dirk shook the boys' hands again and said, "I look forward to working with you guys. Detective Phillips told us you know your stuff." He returned to his chair.

Phillips sat on the edge of the table and glanced at Sammy and Brian. His suit coat was open and his tie pointed down to the opened folder on his lap. "I've brought them up-to-date on what I've found so far. There were no readable fingerprints on the tin box." The detective raised his eyebrows. "Only Brian's prints were on the watch case. But we did find prints on the glass crystal inside. The prints are not on file." Phillips ran his hand back over his hair. "Whoever touched the glass has no criminal record or was ever in the service. Could be Shawn Walker's prints."

Sammy shuffled pages in his notebook. "Did you have time to trace the names of the boarders that the Mellingers gave us—Ray Miller, Dennis Moore, Nancy Gil, and the other two?"

"Yes. Two Ray Millers live in Lancaster County," said Phillips. "I phoned them. They both claimed they never lived in Bird-in-Hand. I also called Dennis Moore. He lives in Ronks. Sells insurance. He admitted being a boarder at the Mellingers' house, but he said he doesn't know anything about the tin box. And there's no trace of Nancy Gil, Andrew Potts, or Susan Taylor."

"The North Carolina Five" represented an enormous amount of information on Walker and what happened twenty-two years ago. Now was the time for Sammy to use this resource. Sammy looked directly at Leon Bradley, the retired cop. "Was there any mention of kidnapping when Shawn Walker vanished?"

Leon thought for a while. "No. There was no ransom note or phone calls at the time. The FBI was never called in on the case. Why do you ask?"

"You said the doctor left a two-million-dollar estate when he died," said Sammy. "If the family had money, that could be a motive for kidnapping."

"Shawn's mother divorced his father a year after this happened," added Leon. "She blamed her husband for her son's disappearance. The doctor died two years later." Leon shook his head and looked at the boys. "The doctor would have said his son was kidnapped if it was true. That would prove to his wife that he was not at fault for his son's disappearance."

"But, if Dr. Walker paid off the kidnappers," said Sammy, "and they killed his son anyway, the wife might be furious with him for not calling in the police. Couldn't the doctor have paid off kidnappers without the police knowing?"

"I guess he could have. But his son never returned. Doesn't that pretty well kill your kidnapping theory?"

Sammy was surprised at the retired cop's lack of vision. "Well, as I said, sometimes even though the ransom is paid, the kidnappers kill the victim so they can't be identified later."

"Well, there's nothing like that on record," snapped Ann Flowers. "If that did happen, the doctor didn't report it to the police." She scratched her ear, took a deep breath, and then added, "So there's no way of knowing."

"Couldn't you check the doctor's bank

account to see if any large amount of money was withdrawn around the time his son disappeared?"

Brian nodded and smiled.

"The North Carolina Five" stared at the teens in silence. Three of them wondered why nobody had thought of that before. The other two thought that it had probably been done and no large withdrawals were noted. Then all eyes settled on Leon Bradley, who had been in charge of the case twenty-two years ago.

His frown announced his embarrassment. "I don't recall having checked that out. You have to understand, kidnapping was not a factor in the investigation. And as I think about it now, I still don't think it happened." Leon glanced at Phillips. "Look, Shawn could have been killed by someone but not as part of a kidnapping plot."

Detective Flowers produced a spiral pad, leaned on the table, and made a note. "Instead of wondering about it, I'll check it out," she said with authority.

Again, looking at Leon Bradley, Sammy asked, "Do you know why Shawn Walker's mother blamed her husband for the son's disappearance?"

Leon glanced at Les Gray then said, "The doctor was very open about the fact that he didn't want his son running around with Les. He said Les was a bad influence on Shawn."

Les quickly defended himself. "The doc never did like me," he said, "and I'll tell you why. I lived on the other side of town. That's why. He was loaded with money and my family had none."

"Were you best friends with Shawn," asked Brian, "like Sammy and I are best friends?"

"You bet we were. We did everything together. When Shawn vanished, it was like losing a member of my own family. That's why I'm here now. I think he's dead, but, well, I'm here. I want to know what happened."

The words, "I think he's dead," rang in Sammy ears. Something else disturbed the teenager. Sammy had learned from John Davenport, a retired Hollywood actor now living in Strasburg, that a person's eyes should reveal his feelings behind his words. The look in Les's eyes didn't match what he had just said.

More questions were asked by those assembled in the conference room. Some were answered, some were not. But they all agreed the investigation would have to continue.

Sammy noted that each of "The North Carolina Five" had his or her reasons for finding Shawn Walker. Les Gray had an emotional bond to his missing best friend. To Ann Flowers, it was a job to be done. Leon Bradley wanted a guilt-free retirement. Art Hansen wanted to write a book with a happy ending—if possible. And Dirk Evans wanted to fulfill a promise he had made to a dying man. He would track down Shawn Walker, dead or alive.

Before the meeting broke up, Art Hansen, the writer, cornered the boys and got the information he needed to confirm and supplement the newspapers' account of the tin box. Dirk Evans, the investigator, made a promise to keep in touch with the teenage detectives to compare notes on the case. Les Gray, Ann Flowers, and Leon Bradley made no attempt to further their relations with the amateur detectives.

When "The North Carolina Five" finally left the room, Brian realized how hungry he was. He glanced at his watch. "Hey, I have to get home and eat and do my homework."

Sammy nodded. "I have to leave, too. Be at my house at seven so we can brainstorm and organize our speech for the elementary children tomorrow."

"Right," said Brian as his empty stomach rushed him out the door.

"Well, what do you think of our visitors?" asked Phillips as he and Sammy stood alone in the room.

"We can use all the help we can get," said Sammy. "Maybe one of them will find Shawn Walker—or the person responsible for his disappearance."

Phillips walked over to a small table and filled his coffee mug. "They're all staying at the Bird-in-Hand Family Inn." He raised his eyebrows. "I hope they don't start bumping into each other. You know what they say about too many cooks."

"Yeah, they spoil the broth," added Sammy with an uneasy feeling.

"Oh, I almost forgot," said Phillips, reaching into his folder. "Here's a picture of Shawn Walker—as he looked twenty-two years ago. You may have this copy."

It was the same pose that appeared in the news article from the tin box. Its detail was better but it didn't help much. "He looks like a homeless person," said Sammy. "His hair's a mess and he has a beard. He didn't care much about his appearance, did he?"

"His father blamed Les Gray for that," said Phillips. "He said Gray made a hippie out of his son."

Sammy shook his head. "It's amazing what twenty-two years can do. Les Gray didn't look like a hippie to me. He was wearing a suit."

"Yes, and I'm sure Shawn won't look like a hippie either—if he's alive out there somewhere."

As Sammy turned to leave, Phillips said, "Oh, by the way, would you and Brian mind having a talk with Dennis Moore, the boarder?" The detective handed a scrap of paper to Sammy. "Here's his address in Ronks. I talked to him on the phone, but you boys have a way of extracting crucial information from a suspect."

"Sure. We can see him tomorrow after school," said Sammy.

"If you don't come up with anything, I'll pay Mr. Moore a personal visit," Phillips added.

When Sammy got to the opened doorway, he spotted a folded slip of paper on the floor. Thinking the paper contained important notes, he stooped and picked it up. His name was on the front. He unfolded the paper and read the hand-printed message. **Don't look for Shawn Walker. He's dead. Don't get involved**.

Sammy turned and looked back. Detective Phillips was busy writing in his folder. "I hate to say this," said Sammy, "but here's another chapter in this case." He handed the note to Phillips.

After reading the short message, Phillips shook his head and frowned. "One of our visitors from North Carolina wants you off this case." He handed the note back to the young detective.

"Wasn't it Les Gray, Shawn Walker's friend, who just said he thought Shawn was dead?" asked Sammy. "He's the only one who said that."

"Yeah, but how many believe he might be dead?" asked Phillips.

All of a sudden, Sammy realized he had another mystery to solve. Which one of "The North Carolina Five" wrote the note and why?

CHAPTER FIVE

B rian read the note again for the fourth time. He had arrived promptly at 6:55 in time for the scheduled brainstorming session in Sammy's bedroom. His prize for being prompt was the paper that Sammy presented to him.

"Oh, my gosh," said Brian. "Someone knows that Shawn Walker is dead, and he wants us to stop looking for the body."

The desk chair squeaked as Sammy leaned back. "One of those five people wrote the note. What we have to figure out is why we pose a threat to that person."

"What do you mean?" asked Brian, placing the note on the desk.

"They're professionals," said Sammy. "As far as they're concerned, we're two teenagers living in Bird-in-Hand who accidentally found a tin box. Why would anyone think we can cause trouble?"

Brian was insulted. "Didn't the newspapers mention the cases we solved and how we help the police? Hey, we're known all over the world by now, I bet."

"Lancaster County, maybe, but not in North Carolina," said Sammy. "To them we're hicks, living in a hick village somewhere in Lancaster County."

Brian didn't want to hear that. He grimaced, turned, and flung himself, face down, across the foot of the bed.

"Why do you have your face buried in the covers? Aren't you supposed to be looking up?" asked Sammy.

"I'm trying a new position. Now if I could only breathe this way," came a muffled voice from the bed.

Sammy waited.

Brian snapped his body around, took a deep breath, and looked at Sammy. "I think I know why we are a threat. Someone thinks we're close to finding Shawn Walker."

"Why would they think that?" asked Sammy.

"The tin box was hidden in the cellar. Right? What if Shawn Walker is buried down there somewhere."

A chill ran through Sammy's body as he thought of the possibility. After all, Brian suspected that something lay hidden behind the stone in the wall—*in the cellar*. He could be right about the body, also.

Sammy gave a nervous laugh. "Are you saying the body is hidden in the wall, too."

Brian jumped from the bed. "No, under the dirt floor."

Sammy rose from behind his desk and headed for the door. "Come on. I know you won't be satisfied until we check it out."

"You, too. Right, Sammy?"

Sammy rushed down the steps. Brian was right. He had to know.

A concrete sidewalk had been laid around the house two months before. Several metal rods, a half inch in diameter and six feet long, used to reinforce the concrete, were left over. Sammy grabbed a rod and a hammer from the shed and joined his friend in the cellar.

Half of the cellar had a concrete floor. The other half was dirt. Sammy knew the wooden steps that led to the outside had the date 1955 carved into the wood. Since the wooden steps rested on top of the concrete floor, the concrete was older. If the body was buried somewhere, it would have to be under the dirt.

"Wouldn't it be easier to remove the dirt with a shovel?" asked Brian, staring at the thin rod.

"We don't have to remove the dirt. I'll hammer this rod down through the dirt. If a body is in the way, the metal rod will hit it."

Sammy positioned the rod in the center of the dirt area and pushed it down. Then he used the hammer to force it deeper into the hard-packed earth. Sammy wiggled the rod each time he drove it deeper to keep it loose. He wanted to be able to withdraw the rod after each hole was made.

On the first attempt, the rod went down four feet without hitting anything. Two feet of the rod was above the dirt. When the boys tried to remove it, it wouldn't budge.

"Oh, oh, now what do we do? Call your father?" asked Brian.

"No, I have an idea," said Sammy, heading for the stairs.

He returned a minute later with lock-grip pliers.

Brian watched as his buddy snapped the pliers onto the rod near the top. Sammy slammed the hammer against the under side of the pliers, driving it and the attached rod upward. After the third hit, the rod was loose enough for Sammy and Brian to pull it out the rest of the way.

For the second attempt, Sammy positioned the rod a foot to the left of the first hole. The rod descended two feet and then stopped.

Sammy tapped the top of the rod again. The rod didn't move any deeper.

The boys looked at each other.

Was this it? Was the body below them?

Using muscle power, the boys were able to pull the rod from the hole.

They tried again six more inches to the left. This time the rod traveled down four feet. The previous attempt had probably struck a stone.

The fourth half-inch hole was made one foot in another direction from the first hole. The rod reached four feet without interference. The boys continued expanding out from the original hole. When the fourteenth hole had been punched into the dirt floor, they stopped. Sammy said he would buy sand to fill the holes.

Both boys were convinced that Shawn Walker's body was not buried in the cellar.

But was it buried somewhere else? Until Detective Phillips connected the Mellingers to Shawn Walker, they decided not to dig up the yard.

———————

Brian Helm was all smiles the next day at school. His homework was done. Sammy and he had planned their presentation for the children, and they would miss the last two periods of the day. The young detectives were to report to the office at 1:30.

As they walked down the hall, eager for their afternoon adventure, a man hurried from the office and exited the building.

Brian grabbed Sammy's arm, "Wasn't that one of the men from North Carolina?"

"Yeah," answered Sammy. "That was Les Gray, Shawn Walker's friend. I wonder what he was doing here?"

At that moment another man came rushing from the office toward them.

"Here comes Mr. Baksa. Let's ask him," said Brian.

The principal's face was flushed, his eyes weary. The burden of his job was unkind. There were schedules, countless meetings, emergencies— all problems he was expected to solve. But he managed to smile. "You boys ready for your assembly program? I want to be sure to get you back in time for the buses."

"We're ready," said Sammy. "The man that just left the office, I think we met him at the police station yesterday. Was he from North Carolina?"

Mr. Baksa hesitated and frowned as if debating whether to reveal school business to two students. Finally he said, "This will be of interest to you, but let's not waste time. I'll tell you in the car."

The principal glanced at the boys through the rearview mirror as they headed for the Smoketown Elementary School. "You went to the Smoketown Elementary School, didn't you?"

"Yeah, kindergarten to sixth grade," said Brian. He stretched his neck to see if the school was in sight yet. He was really looking forward to this visit.

"You were going to tell us about the man back at school," said Sammy, hoping he wasn't being too pushy.

"He *is* the man you met yesterday. Mr. Gray. He wanted to know whether you and Brian went to our school. He asked a lot of questions about you boys. He also asked if the school records showed whether a Shawn Walker ever had children enrolled in our schools."

"Boy, that's a long shot," said Sammy. "In the last twenty-two years, there could have been a hundred Walkers all over Lancaster County."

"I knew from the newspapers that Shawn Walker was the missing college student," said the principal. "I told him he would have to go to our administration building to check the records."

"Shawn Walker and Mr. Gray were close friends," said Sammy. "Now that the watch has been found, he's going all out to find . . ." Sammy touched Brian's shoulder. "Yesterday at the police station, Mr. Gray said he thought his friend was dead. Why is he now trying to find him?"

"Yeah," said Brian. "He should be trying to prove he's dead."

"If I was Mr. Gray, I'd be talking to Dennis Moore, the boarder," said Sammy. "He's our only hope of being the person who put the tin box into the wall."

"Maybe he already talked to him," said Brian.

"We're going to see Mr. Moore after school today," said Sammy. "We can find out if he had a visit from Mr. Gray."

Mr. Baksa found an open parking space in front of the school. As the trio walked from the car toward the front entrance, Sammy was aware of eyes watching from a parked car.

"Look," said Sammy, pointing. "Look who followed us!"

It was Les Gray.

CHAPTER SIX

L es Gray made no effort to get out of his car. He just sat there staring.

Feeling uncomfortable, the three entered the school, checked in at the office, and were escorted to the all-purpose room.

The classes quickly filed in. Fifth and sixth graders sat in chairs in the back. The third and fourth graders sat on the floor in front. The teachers introduced themselves to the teen-age detectives and to Mr. Baksa, then they retreated to the back of the room.

Mr. Baksa introduced himself and Sammy and Brian to the children. He then stepped aside and let the boys run the show.

Sammy started by detailing their first case, The Quilted Message. Brian next, dramatically described how he faced great danger when he was grabbed and held hostage in their second case, Bird in the Hand.

Sammy followed with a brief description of

how he and Brian investigated "accidents" happening to an old farmer in the case of Amish Justice. He told how a toy train, brought to Strasburg by a retiring Hollywood actor, held a secret that was linked back to World War II.

He introduced the importance of brainstorming. "Asking questions and kicking around ideas can open up new avenues of thinking," he said. "It helps you look at things differently from a new viewpoint."

He went on to explain how it's important to use all your senses when looking for clues. He and Brian told how they had found certain clues and how these clues were used to pinpoint the guilty person.

Finally, Brian was in his glory as he recalled how he found the sealed tin box. Standing tall and in a deep voice (which caused him to cough several times) he told of the gold pocket watch and the twenty-two-year-old news article.

Then came time for questions.

"Do you make a lot of money?" asked a boy in front.

"No," said Sammy. "We don't charge for our work. We do it for the experience."

A girl raised her hand. She pointed to Brian. "My mother knows your mother."

"That's nice," replied Brian, wondering what the question was.

A girl in the back asked, "Do you think the guy is alive? You know, the guy that disappeared."

"We have no idea at this time," said Sammy. "Remember this case is new. We're still working on it."

"I think he's dead. That's what my dad said," came a voice from the side.

"I think he's alive," said a snickering voice. "He probably ran away from his wife."

"The person we're talking about is Shawn Walker," said Sammy. "He was a nineteen-year-old college student. He wasn't married. But that shows you're thinking. You bring up a good point. He could have run away."

Brian watched as the boy sat up straight and lost his frivolous attitude. Brian remembered when he had been the class clown.

Sammy continued. "What other reasons might Shawn Walker have had for running away?"

Many hands went up.

"He wanted to be a movie star so he went to Hollywood."

"He didn't like college so he ran away."

"He beat up people, and he stole a radio, and the police came after him, and he crashed his car, and somebody took his dog, and . . . and so he ran away."

"This may sound way out, but maybe he wanted to explore the world."

"His mother made him clean up his room."

"I saw you last week at the shopping mall."

"Maybe he did something wrong, like rob a bank, and he didn't want to get caught."

"He didn't like the way he looked so he ran away to have plastic surgery."

"He had a girlfriend up here. His parents didn't like her so he came here and got married."

"Those are all good ideas," said Sammy. "And one of them could be the very reason why Shawn Walker vanished. You've given Brian and me something to think about. Thank you."

The waving hand in back could not escape from being noticed. Brian looked at his watch and feeling very much like a teacher, he said, "We have time for one more question. Okay, you in the back."

The sixth-grade girl adjusted her glasses and raised her eyebrows. "The newspaper said you found the tin box in a wall in your house. But it didn't say what wall. And you didn't tell us today. I just wanted to know what wall it was. You know, where you found it."

Sammy and Brian looked at each other.

"I'll answer that," said Sammy. "We were told by the police not to mention the exact location of the box. They don't want the public to know exactly where the box was found." Sammy saw the puzzled look on their faces. "Now let me tell you why. The police like to keep certain facts about their cases secret. Sometimes people confess to things that aren't true. So if a person comes in and says, 'I'm the one who put the tin box in the wall,' the police will ask, 'Which wall?' If the person doesn't know which wall, then that person is lying."

A fifth grader asked, "Why would somebody say they did something when they didn't?"

"Well," said Sammy. "Sometimes people are sick. They're out of touch with reality. Some people are lonely. They want attention. They'll confess to anything just to have someone to talk to. Now that sounds dumb to you and me, but not to the people who are sick or lonely."

A teacher raised her hand. "So only you, Brian, and the police know the exact spot where the box was found."

"My mother and father know," said Sammy. He glanced at Brian, saw the expression, and added, "And Brian's parents know."

Suddenly a teacher appeared in front and said, "Our time is up. Let's thank Sammy Wilson and Brian Helm for being here today."

The children applauded, talked among themselves, and stood to return to their classrooms.

On the way back to the high school, something bothered Sammy. It wasn't that Les Gray's car was gone from the parking lot when they left the building. It was something said at the assembly program. His subconscious mind had picked up on an important clue. Now if his conscious mind could only grasp it. He decided not to think of it.

"That was fun," said Brian. "Are we going to do more schools like that, Mr. Baksa?"

"Yes, as soon as I can make the arrangements," said the principal.

Sammy's eyes sparkled and a half-smile appeared. Not because of what Mr. Baksa had just said, but as a result of a thought that suddenly materialized. He reran the image of Les Gray at the high school and in the parked car. He drew the photograph of Shawn Walker from his shirt pocket and handed it over the seat to Mr. Baksa. "That's Shawn Walker twenty-two years ago. Ever see anyone who resembles him?"

Transferring his eyes back and forth from the road to the picture, the principal took quick glances at the photo. He shook his head. "He looks rough around the edges. If you shave the beard, cut the hair, and add twenty-two years, he could be anybody." He handed the picture back to Sammy without taking his eyes off the road.

Sammy returned the photo to his pocket. "Sometimes you can identify people from old photographs by the shape of their ears. They say the contour of ears never changes. It's too bad Shawn Walker's long hair covers his ears."

"I was just thinking," said Brian. "If they find his body, how will they know it's him?"

"From dental records, most likely," said Sammy.

Mr. Baksa returned the boys to the high school in time for them to catch their bus home. They had not encountered Les Gray along the way. It made Sammy wonder what Mr. Gray was doing now that he was "absent from school."

The events of the day gave the young detectives a lot to talk about. But brainstorming would have to wait until that evening. First, they had to pay a visit to Dennis Moore in Ronks. The Mellingers and he were the only live link they had to the tin box. Since the Mellingers appeared innocent, would it be Dennis Moore who held all the answers?

CHAPTER SEVEN

The Village of Ronks was one mile from Bird-in-Hand. Houses and businesses lined Ronks Road, its main street. Behind, on both sides, lay miles and miles of farmland.

Sammy and Brian checked the number on the mailbox with the address on the paper. It matched.

"I'll beat you up to the house," said Brian as he headed his bike toward an incline.

The old brick house stood up from the road by a high stone wall. The house sat back about fifty feet with steps leading up to the front lawn. With some effort, the teen-age detectives pedaled up the slanted driveway.

A man in his early forties was raking leaves and smoking a cigar. He wore khaki pants and a sweatshirt. His plump face puffed out smoke as he pivoted in a complete circle and allowed the rake's fingers to do the walking. The cigar ashes that dropped onto the dry leaves went unnoticed.

"Are you Dennis Moore?" asked Sammy as he and Brian lowered their bikes to the grass.

The man continued raking like he was a man on a mission.

Sammy tried again. "Are you . . ."

The man stopped, took the cigar from his mouth, and glanced at the boys. "Yep." The cigar returned to his mouth as the rake again pawed at the leaves.

"I'm Sammy Wilson and this is Brian Helm."

The man stopped, freed the cigar from the clutches of his teeth, and said, "Dirk Evans, a private investigator, was here today. He said you boys would be around. And I'll tell you what I told him. I don't know anything about an old tin box with a watch inside."

"Mr. Evans is gathering information about a man missing for twenty-two years," said Sammy.

"He showed me a picture. It was the guy who owned the pocket watch."

"Shawn Walker," said Brian.

"I don't know the guy. I never saw the watch," said Dennis as he put the rake and the cigar back to work. "There's only one way to rake leaves. You stand in one spot, swivel, and rake the leaves toward you. Then move to another spot and do the same. That way you're not raking the same leaves over and over." He demonstrated for the boys, ending up with several small piles of leaves instead of one large heap.

Here is a man who accounts for his every move, thought Sammy. He's methodical. He plans his actions ahead of time. He fits the mold of someone who would seal a tin box with wax to preserve its contents.

Dennis Moore walked toward his visitors and continued his lecture. "You see, it's important to conserve energy."

Brian looked at the man's bulging stomach. He could see where Mr. Moore was storing the energy.

A white stream of smoke floated up from a leaf pile.

Brian pointed and yelled, "Hey! You have a fire back there!"

Dennis Moore looked, remained calm, and made no attempt to smother the fire. He was going to allow it to burn itself out. "There, you see that? We're going to have a small fire now instead of a large one."

You wouldn't have any fire at all, thought Brian, if you didn't smoke that dumb cigar.

The man's cool, real cool, thought Sammy. He saw the look in Mr. Moore's blue eyes. The man was enjoying the destruction of the dry leaves, knowing that that same fire was also destroying the living green grass below.

Moore dropped his cigar and crushed it beneath his shoe. "As I said, I read the papers. You're the kids who found the box."

"You're a very smart man, Mr. Moore. But I bet you don't know where we found it," said

Sammy, willing to put all his eggs in one question. A man like Mr. Moore felt superior to other people. He would welcome a challenge. So Sammy was appealing to his vanity, hoping to catch him in the trap.

"Sure I know where you found it," he said, taking off his glasses. He inspected the lenses. "I don't know where all this dirt comes from."

Brian shook his head and thought to himself, The poor guy can't see the forest for the cigar smoke.

Moore pulled a tissue from his pocket. He huffed and puffed on each lens, and wiped them clean. In a smooth maneuver, he completed the ceremony by carefully fitting the glasses back onto his face. "You found the box in a wall in the house somewhere, I believe. The papers said so. I read a lot, you know. Best thing you can do, no matter what you want to be in life. Read, read, read."

Sammy agreed, but was disappointed that Mr. Moore hadn't taken the bait he laid out for him. "I understand from Detective Ben Phillips that you rented a room from the Mellingers back in the seventies."

"Yep, two years I lived there, 1977 and 1978."

"Do you remember seeing a pocket watch or a Hershey candy box lying around the house anywhere?" asked Sammy.

"There you go with that watch and box again. No. The only metal box I remember seeing was a large red cookie tin where the Mellingers kept their bills."

"The police found fingerprints inside the watch," said Sammy. "Do you mind if we take a sample of your prints?"

Dennis Moore's eyes glanced up and to his right. The movement was not missed by Sammy. Mr. Moore was trying to remember something. Something from his past. Would he have a reason for not wanting his prints on record? Or—were they already on file?

"No, no, I don't mind," came the unexpected response.

Sammy whipped out a clean piece of plastic he had prepared beforehand. He held the plastic by the edges. "Here, take a hold of this with your fingers and thumb." Sammy was surprised that Dennis Moore showed no hesitation as he applied his prints to the plastic. The amateur detective just as quickly returned the fingerprint sample to an envelope.

"Ever been to Greensboro, North Carolina?" asked Brian.

"Nope, don't believe so," said Moore as he looked back at the smoldering leaves. "Do you think that Walker guy is still alive?"

"I sure hope so," said Sammy. "What do you think happened to him?"

"Well, since you found his watch in the wall, he put it there so he's alive. That's not hard to figure out."

"Then why do you think he just up and ran away from Greensboro?" asked Sammy.

Mr. Moore rubbed his two-day whiskers. "First thing I thought of when I read the paper was that he owed a lot of money. You know, gambling. That sort of thing."

"Maybe you could help us. Let's assume that Shawn Walker was killed by someone and made it look like he disappeared. How do you think it was done?"

"If it was me, and he was dead, I'd cover him with leaves."

"Is that all?" asked Brian.

Dennis Moore's eyes sparkled. "No, then I'd set the leaves on fire."

CHAPTER EIGHT

"Do you think Mr. Moore was pulling our legs?" asked Brian as he wiggled across the foot of the bed and focused his eyes on the ceiling. "I can't believe he said that."

Sammy smiled. "Of course, he was pulling our legs. He was smart enough to know that we knew he was kidding. That's why he said it."

Brian adjusted his body to fit into the cavity already formed in the mattress. "But if he's smart enough to know we would believe he was kidding, maybe he told us the truth."

Sammy snapped his head from behind his computer to glance at his friend. "Brian, that's a great possibility. I'm surprised you thought of it." Sammy wanted to take the words back as soon as he said them, but it was too late.

Brian sat up. "So you think I'm dumb. Is that it?"

"No, that's not it," said Sammy. "With all we've been through today, it's a wonder we can think at all. We were at school. We saw Les Gray. We saw him later at Smoketown. We interacted with the elementary children. When we got home, we rode to Ronks and talked to Dennis Moore. It's a wonder we can still think. That's all I'm saying."

Before Brian could respond, Mr. Wilson called from downstairs. Sammy was wanted on the phone.

When Sammy returned, Brian was in a new frame of mind. "That was Detective Phillips. Detective Ann Flowers checked with the Greensboro bank. Doctor Walker withdrew twenty-five thousand dollars a day or two after his son disappeared."

"Does that mean he was kidnapped and then killed after the payoff?" asked Brian.

"Looks that way," said Sammy.

Brian was puzzled. "But what's his pocket watch doing up here in Bird-in-Hand twenty-two years later?"

Sammy sat again at his desk. "That's what we'll have to find out."

Mrs. Wilson stepped into the bedroom. "Here's an envelope for you." She knew that an opened door allowed her to enter the private world of the Sammy and Brian Detective Enterprises. "A girl dropped it off in the store a little while ago. She was pretty, too." She sniffed at the envelope in mock suspicion and handed the letter to her son. She retreated from the room sporting a mother's smile.

"Thanks, Mom," yelled Sammy as he opened the sealed envelope.

Brian hopped from the bed. "So you have a girlfriend," said Brian. "Are you sure that's not for me?" Brian could see that his friend was in no mood for humor.

After several seconds and deep in thought, Sammy spun the letter around so it settled on the desk in front of Brian. "Here, read this, but don't touch it. It might have fingerprints."

I am being blackmailed by Les Gray. Please find a way to stop him without him finding out that I told you. Please keep this to yourself. I don't want anyone else to know. I am to meet Les Gray at Borders Book Shop near Park City Mall at 5 o'clock Wednesday.

Shawn Walker

"Wow! Shawn Walker is alive!" said Brian. "So the plot thickens."

Sammy examined the envelope. It contained only his name typed on the front.

"Wednesday, that's tomorrow," said Brian. "Gee, we can go there and we'll meet Shawn Walker . . . and . . ."

Sammy was shaking his head. He picked up the note by the edges. "How do we know that Shawn Walker really wrote this?" His eyebrows lifted, releasing the full potential of his blue eyes. "It could have been written by someone who wants us to believe Shawn Walker is still alive."

"Yeah, that's right," said Brian. Then as an afterthought, he asked, "Why would someone want us to think Shawn Walker's alive?"

"That's a good question," said Sammy. "Let's throw that idea around. Who would benefit from Walker being alive?"

Brian resumed his official brainstorming position on the bed. "Maybe Les Gray. He knows there's two million dollars in the bank waiting for Shawn Walker to claim it. He probably wants some of it."

"What good is that to Les Gray if Shawn's really dead?" asked Sammy.

Brian shrugged at the ceiling. "I don't know. It just sounded like a good idea."

Sammy walked to the window and looked down at Main Street. The tourists were still in full bloom even in October. He noticed they weren't all tourists. He turned back to Brian. "Whoever killed him would also want us to believe he's still living."

"How about the writer, Art Hansen," said Brian. "Wouldn't it make a better story if Shawn Walker was still alive?"

"Yes, that's true. The arrival of this note also 'thickens the plot' as you said earlier. That would make for a better story."

"Do you think Art Hansen is behind the note?" asked Brian. "Maybe he sent the girl to deliver it."

Sammy frowned and reread the note. He puckered his lips and said slyly, "I just thought of someone who would benefit from Mr. Walker being alive."

"Who?" asked Brian, concentrating on the ceiling.

"Shawn Walker. Remember, there's two million dollars waiting for him in Greensboro, North Carolina."

"But if he's alive he would have the money by now," said Brian.

"Not if he doesn't know it's there," said Sammy. "Now, let's go back to our original question. Why would someone want us to believe he's alive? What if someone wanted the two million so he pretended to be Shawn Walker?"

"Yeah, but he would have to prove that he was the missing Walker," said Brian. "How would he do that?"

"I don't know, but I'm sure a con man might try it. But I'll tell you, Brian, I suspect the real Shawn Walker is alive and living here among us."

Brian raised his head from the bed. "Yeah? Who is it?"

"I said, I *suspect.* Remember, we don't accuse anyone . . ."

"Yeah, I know," said Brian, focusing again on the ceiling. "We don't accuse anyone until we have proof."

Sammy sat behind his desk, leaned back, and took a deep breath. "If the real Walker is alive, why didn't he come and talk to us in person instead of writing the note? Better still, why doesn't he go to the police if he's being blackmailed?"

"He doesn't want his identity known," answered Brian.

"If that's true, then he won't show up at tomorrow's meeting at Borders with Les Gray."

"Right," said Brian, "because we'll be there and we would see him."

Sammy grinned. "And if somebody does show up and claims to be Shawn Walker, he won't be."

"Oh, I'm so confused by all this," said Brian. "And . . . and . . . anyway, how does he expect us to help him from being blackmailed?"

"Brian, are you saying we're dumb?" replied Sammy, trying to cancel out his earlier remark to Brian.

"Okay, we're even. Now how are we going to handle our meeting with Les Gray tomorrow at Borders Book Shop?"

Sammy rubbed his eyes, locked his fingers behind his head, and glanced at the bulletin board on the side wall. What was the blackmail all about? he wondered. What information could Les Gray have that enabled him to blackmail Shawn Walker? How could Brian and he find out?

The super sleuth's eyes locked onto a news article pinned to the bulletin board. The headline read: THE FRIGHT TRAIN ROLLS INTO STRASBURG. It was a news item that detailed Sammy and Brian's investigation and final solution of a mystery that surrounded a toy train. The wheels were turning as Sammy relived part of that case.

Brian knew when to keep quiet. He raised his head from time to time to check on Sammy's progress. The completion of the plan would be announced by a slight smile on Sammy's lips and a sparkle of satisfaction radiating from his blue eyes.

On his fifth head-raising, Brian saw the signs and smiled. A new plan had been born. He wondered whether Sammy would reveal the plan to him in all its details. Probably not. Sammy had been known to withhold details of a plan from Brian. "For the success of the plan," Sammy would say later.

Brian sat up in bed, allowing his short legs to dangle over the edge. "What's our plan of attack?"

"First, we have to prove that Shawn Walker is being blackmailed by Les Gray. Next, we need to break up the blackmail without letting Mr. Gray know that Shawn Walker told us."

"How are we going to do that?" asked Brian.

Sammy stood. "We're going to visit with Mr. Gray at the book store tomorrow."

Brian stood at attention and saluted. "What are my orders, chief?"

Sammy rolled his eyes. "When we start talking to Mr. Gray, I will try to find out where he parked his car. Then I want you to excuse yourself and leave. You saw his car at the school so you know what it looks like. It will have a North Carolina plate on it. Go to his car and get the license number. Look in the car window. Check for anything unusual in the car then I'll meet you in front of the store."

"Right, chief," said Brian, again saluting. "I can handle that. It's a dangerous mission, but I will gladly put my life on the line. I will sweat, bleed, and suffer." Brian drew his face up tight. "I will go gladly into the unknown and face the dangers that linger there." He lifted an imaginary trench coat collar. "And why do I do it? I'll tell you why." He placed his left foot forward, stood stiff, and tilted his chin upward. "It's to keep Lancaster County safe. Yes, safe from criminals, slime balls, villains, bad guys, and naughty people."

"Are you finished, Brian?" asked Sammy, wanting to cut short his friend's melodramatics.

"No, I have just one more thing to ask."

"And what's that?"

"May I bring my mommy along with me?"

Sammy grinned. "That's funny, Brian. Real funny."

"Gee, thanks," said Brian. "That's what I'm here for, *just to entertain you.*" His tone was bitter, the words falling hard on Sammy's ears.

"Okay, what's your problem?" asked Sammy. "I know by the way you're acting that you're mad at me."

"Hey, I know you. Remember me? I'm your

old buddy. You're holding something back from me. Right, Sammy? I mean, there's more to your scheme."

"It's for the good of the plan," answered Sammy.

"Oh, great! You usually wait until after it's over to tell me that," said Brian.

Sammy had to push some buttons to defuse his friend. "Brian, you have a talent I don't have."

Brian's ears perked up. The hurt was pushed aside.

"You have the ability to come up with the unexpected. I count on that when we're involved in a case. You can improvise when you're put on the spot. You've demonstrated that many times. And I'm counting on your innate ability to help solve this case. I wouldn't trust anyone else." Sammy thought he'd stop while he was ahead.

Brian smiled. "Innate ability. I have that? You never told me that before."

"Well, you've got it," said Sammy. "There's no doubt about that."

"Innate ability," Brian repeated. "How long do you think I've had it?"

"Probably all your life," answered Sammy, wondering whether he had pushed a button or created a hole in a dam.

With a thoughtful expression, Brian asked, "Do you have a dictionary I can use?"

Sammy grinned and pointed to one of the

many book shelves that lined one bedroom wall.

The muted traffic sounds coming from the street below reminded Sammy of two things. He had a phone call to make. That would wait until Brian went home. And the other . . . He went to the window and again glanced down at the tourists treading their way in and out of the village shops. His eyes didn't miss much. With a distant look on his face, he returned to his desk. The man in the shadows across the street was still there, watching the house.

CHAPTER NINE

The sky was gray, leaking a light mist, teasing the water-hungry crops growing within eyesight of the shopping center. Field corn and the pumpkins would welcome a healthy downpour.

Mr. Wilson dropped the boys off at Borders Book Shop. He had his own shopping to do and promised to pick the boys up an hour later.

Sammy scanned the nearby parking areas. He saw no car resembling Les Gray's car. He glanced at his watch. 4:50. He peered through the store window into the coffee café. Some of the tables were occupied with people in various postures, reading books, magazines, and newspapers. Les Gray was alone at one of the tables with his head tilted down, reading a newspaper.

"Come on, Brian, follow me," said Sammy as he opened the door, went past the service desk, and headed for the café. He picked up two magazines from a nearby rack and followed the aromatic smells to the counter.

Both boys bought a Turkey Hill iced tea and sat at the empty table directly behind Les Gray. They propped the magazines up to shield themselves, should Mr. Gray turn around.

"Good. He hasn't seen us," whispered Sammy. "We'll wait awhile and see what happens."

"We should have Joyce Myers with us," whispered Brian. "She could take some pictures." He took a sip of his drink and glanced around, expecting to see Joyce's camera poking out from behind a book display.

At one of the tables, a woman was reading from a picture book to her four-year-old daughter. A college student at another table was taking notes and drinking coffee.

From a pile of three western sagas on his table, an old man was deciding which book to buy. He hardly qualified as a person who could afford a book. Homeless, was a word that came to mind. He wore an old-fashioned, battered hat and a prospector's outfit straight from the Gold Rush of 1849. His unkempt beard and broad, bushy mustache covered most of his wrinkled face.

The man read the first page of each book. He then stood, adjusted his suspenders, and slid the books from the table. Instead of leaving the café area, he shuffled to another table—the table in front of Sammy and Brian.

Les Gray's table.

He placed the books on the newspaper, interfering with Gray's concentration. He slid into the chair opposite.

The unexpected action startled Les Gray. He looked up, trying to recognize the man. He didn't.

"I've been watching you for a long time," said the old man in a whisper. "You've been following Sammy Wilson and Brian Helm." The old man grabbed Les Gray's wrist and squeezed. "I want it stopped. Now. You understand?"

Sammy and Brian heard the conversation—their names. "Do you know that guy?" whispered Brian.

The young detective leaned close to Brian's ear. "I never saw him before. But he evidently knows us."

Gray jerked his arm away and glanced right and left to see if anyone took notice of what was happening. No one seemed to notice. Keeping his voice low, Gray turned to the old man. "Look, don't threaten me. I'm not following those pretend detectives. What I do is none of your business. So beat it."

The old man was unfazed by the scolding. He scratched his whiskers, pulled his hat lower, and leaned forward. "I know about your past and the blackmail," he whispered.

The words took Gray by surprise. "Who are you? Are you from back home, North Carolina? Did Shawn send you?"

"I'm Henry Schnobel, the Third," replied the old man in a sarcastic tone. "No one sent me. I'm here because I'm here. But for your own satisfaction, let's say I overheard a conversation."

"What do you want, *Henry Schnobel, the Third*?" asked Gray, returning the sarcasm.

"I want in on the blackmail," said the old man, maintaining a whisper. "I want to be your partner, fifty fifty."

Sammy and Brian continued to listen. "I wished we had a tape recorder," said Brian.

"Sh," whispered Sammy.

Gray pushed the books toward the old geezer. "Take your books and get out of here. You're mad," he said in a harsh whisper. "Why would I want a partner?"

The old man's right hand probed further under the table. "Because I have a gun pointed at your belly button. And unless you want that button replaced with a zipper, you better consider me the friend you've got in Pennsylvania." A smile broke through the hairs on the old man's face.

Beads of perspiration formed on Gray's forehead at the mention of the word "gun." Without turning completely around, he took a quick look to see if anyone was hearing their conversation. No one was. Evidently nothing was unusual about two men having a discussion in the café.

"And, if you need any further convincing," said the old man, "you see those two big gents outside pretending to be selecting books from the bargain table?"

Gray glanced at the window. "Yeah."

"Unless I give them the signal otherwise, they have orders to take you around the back of the store to your car and break a couple of bones."

"Did you hear that, Brian?" whispered Sammy. "His car's in back of the store. Go. You know what to do."

Brian held the magazine to his face and walked to the rack. He replaced the magazine and headed for the door. Sammy hoped for the best and again turned his attention to the conversation at the table in front of him.

"There's no need for physical violence," said Gray. "Okay, you get half. I'm to get fifty thousand. That's twenty-five thousand apiece."

The old timer knew that Les Gray was too scared to lie. "When do you get the money?"

"I'm to get the money Friday. I'll meet you in the Barnes and Noble coffee café Friday at five o'clock in the afternoon."

"Well, another bookstore," said the old man. "That's on Fruitville Pike. Right?"

Les nodded. "Yeah, I think so."

The old man inched his face closer. "I'll be there. And no double-cross. Your friends from North Carolina won't appreciate the fact that you not only located your friend without telling them, but that you're blackmailing him. Plus, my 'boys' will be trailing you day and night." He sat back and grinned. "And they love to break bones."

"D—D—Don't worry," said Les, his voice quivering. "You'll get your m—money."

"You bet I will, and that twenty-five thousand is going to bring me two hundred thousand in two months."

"What do you mean?" asked Gray.

"Let's just say that I have other partners who make investments."

"What kind of investments?" asked Gray, a man who had an interest in financial dealings.

"I can't say."

"We're partners. Can't you tell me?"

The old man sat sideways on his chair and crossed his legs. "No, I'll get in trouble if I say anything."

"You can at least tell me in what you're investing," said Gray.

The old timer glanced around. "Look, this is just between you and me. My nephew works for GMU Tri-Cepters, out of Massachusetts."

"You mean that large—"

"Yep, that's it. My nephew is in charge of locating potential areas for building growth. He knows beforehand the real estate that is under consideration."

"So?"

"Let's just say that my brothers, sisters, aunts and uncles, and nephews and nieces know the exact piece of property here in Lancaster that's going to be acquired in two months. Eight of us put up fifty thousand each to buy the land, and then we resell it to GMU Tri-Cepters for two million. That's one million six hundred thousand dollars profit, divided by eight, equals two hundred thousand dollars for each of us. Not a bad investment in two months time, huh?"

"What piece of land are we talking about?" asked Gray.

"We're not talking about any piece of land," said the old man. "You think I'm stupid? Look, as a partner, I told you the investment. That's all you get."

Gray nudged closer to the old man. "Any chance I can get in on the GMU Tri-Cepters investment?"

"Nope. I have eight investors. I'm keeping the money in the family."

"They all solid? I mean, they all can come up with their fifty thousand?"

"Yep," said the old timer. "Most will borrow from the bank or take out a second mortgage. I hate to cash in my bonds, so when I stumbled onto your blackmail scheme, I thought I'd join in." His fingers clamped around Gray's wrist again. "Remember, no double-cross or I go to the police. You understand?"

Gray glanced sideways at the window. "Your two goons are gone."

"They're not gone," said the old man. "You just can't see them. I gave them the signal that everything was okay in here." He applied more pressure to Gray's wrist. "Was I wrong?"

"No, I understand. You'll get your money."

"Okay, Barnes and Noble Friday at five. And if you're not there, you're not going to be anywhere." The hardened, senior citizen stood, pulled a red and blue handkerchief from his pants, and blew his nose. "The smell of money always makes my nose run." Having said that, he grabbed his three western novels and trotted off, disappearing through one of the many book aisles.

<hr>

Outside, Brian enjoyed the gloom of the misty atmosphere. It was secret agent weather. The light drizzle made his hair curly. He hated curls, but the thrill of the mission was worth the sacrifice.

The car wasn't hard to find. It was parked near the back wall. However, no assignment was taken lightly by Helm, Brian Helm, secret agent double-oh-seven and a half. Secret agent Helm stalked the premises, noting the layout of the parking area. A man with his back to him was throwing trash into a dumpster. A man and a woman hurried from their car and headed for the Olive Garden next door.

As a secret agent he had to assume many roles. At that very moment he was . . . a young lad, strolling through the lot . . . looking for something he lost. Humming no particular tune, he hunched over and scanned the macadam around him. He meandered toward Les Gray's car, picking up a wet stone here and a wet piece of paper there. He discarded the items as he neared the car.

The hum changed to a whistle as secret agent Helm slid a pen and note pad from his pocket. Turning his back to anyone who might be spying, he jotted down the North Carolina license plate number. He then secured the notebook back to the safety of his pocket.

Next came the most dangcrous part—spying through the car window. No detail was too small to uncover when you're on a high-level secret assignmcnt. Just one clue was all secret agent Helm needed to send Les Gray, blackmailer at large, to jail.

Brian sneaked around to the far side of the car and peeked in through the window. The front seats were clean. He moved to the back window, but before he could look in, he heard a clicking noise.

Someone had unlocked the car doors!

He looked right. He looked left. The wall was behind him. No place to hide. The next car was too far away.

He was trappcd!

From fifty feet away, Les Gray had used his remote keyless entry to unlock the car doors. The drizzle had turned into a light rain, and Gray had no umbrella. He made a dash for his car. He opened the door and slid into the driver's seat. At the same time another individual entered the passenger side of the car.

The intruder wore a ski mask.

"Please stop looking for me," warned the strained whispered voice. "I don't want to be found. If you and the others from North Carolina continue your search, I won't be responsible for what happens."

"But, but, I—" said Gray.

The masked man interrupted. "You heard me say, *please*, this time. Next time you won't be able to hear me say anything. You got the message? Go back home!"

Les Gray nodded.

"And the same goes for you, too, Brian," said the masked stranger as his hand reached over the seat and grabbed a handful of wet T-shirt.

As a last-second attempt to escape, poor Brian had opened the rear door and had thrown himself on the back floor of the car. The upward pull on his shirt persuaded him to give up his hiding place. He rose to his knees, his hands gripping a head rest. His faced slowly inched into view. He was now face to face with Les Gray and a ski mask. He shrugged. "I came in to get out of the rain," he said sheepishly.

CHAPTER TEN

"But Les Gray could have driven off with you in the car if the masked guy hadn't shown up," said Phillips as the two super sleuths sat in Detective Phillips's office.

"Hey, I had to hide somewhere," said Brian. He looked at Sammy. "I was using my *innate ability*—remember?"

Phillips sat back and stretched his arms over his head. "Okay, you told me about the masked fellow who indicated that he was Shawn Walker. Sounds to me that it was. What do you think?"

"I'm not so sure," said Sammy, sliding the note from the other Shawn Walker over the desk to Phillips. "You might want to check that for prints after you read it."

Phillips read the note without touching it. When he finished, he looked up. "We have Shawn Walkers all over the place now. This doesn't sound like the same guy."

"Right," said Sammy. "Why would he write this letter asking for our help and then show up himself in a mask to threaten Les Gray?"

Phillips looked thoughtfully at the note. "According to this message, he is being blackmailed. So you were at Borders to sit in on the blackmail meeting." He pointed to the typed name on the note. "Did this Shawn Walker show up?"

Before Sammy could answer, Detective Marvin Wetzel stuck his head in the door. "There's a man out here wanting to see Sammy and Brian."

"Who is he?" asked Phillips.

"Well, he looks like 'Yosemite Sam.'" Wetzel lifted his eyebrows. "If you know what I mean. He said his name is Henry Schnobel, the Third."

"That's the man who sat at the table with Mr. Gray," said Brian. "He had a gun and he threatened—"

"He's part of why we were at the bookstore," interrupted Sammy.

Phillips gave a nod to Wetzel. "Search him for weapons then send him in here."

"No weapons," said Detective Wetzel seconds later as he ushered the old man into the office. "Want me to stick around?" asked Wetzel.

Phillips took a quick look at "Henry Schnobel, the Third" and shook his head at Wetzel who then returned to the front desk.

Brian stood, squeezed past Sammy, and moved to the far side of the desk. This sudden voluntary action wasn't done as a courtesy but more as a survival tactic. Brian was ready to duck behind the desk should the old man became violent.

The senior citizen was eager to sit in the folding chair vacated by Brian. He sat back, gave his hat a tip with his thumb, and looked at Sammy. "They don't know do they?" he asked.

"No," said Sammy.

"Is it okay if I make myself comfortable?" asked the old timer as he removed his hat.

Phillips, still perplexed by the pathetic-looking character, nodded.

The old man placed his hat on the desk. He removed his wig. He removed his mustache and beard. He stepped out of the old rugged pants and shirt. Underneath, he wore a knit shirt and jeans. "Ah," he said as he glanced at Brian. "It's good to be myself again." His voice had lost its hard edge.

"It's John Davenport, the actor," said Brian.

"I'm disappointed," said Phillips. "I thought it was going to be another Shawn Walker. Tell me, did any other Shawn Walker show up at the bookstore?"

Brian, who was still puzzled at the old man's transformation into John Davenport, pointed and said, "No, but he did."

The seventy-four-year-old actor stood and shook hands with Detective Phillips. "Hi, I'm John Davenport."

"Yes, I recognize you," said Phillips. "I've seen your movies. You're retired now and live in Strasburg, I believe."

"Yes, that's right," said the actor.

"You want to tell me what this is all about?" asked Phillips.

Brian gave Sammy the old evil eye. "Looks like someone forgot to tell me something."

John Davenport winked at Sammy then faced Phillips. "I got a call from Sammy last night. He asked me if I would be interested in doing an unadvertised bit of acting at Borders Book Shop. He explained about the case you're working on and described the note he had received about the blackmail. His plan was for me to approach Gray as a crook myself and find out if he was really blackmailing Shawn Walker. If he was, I was to put the squeeze on Les Gray for part of the blackmail money." The actor pulled a micro tape player from his back pocket. "Here, you can listen to the whole conversation with Les Gray."

"You taped it?" asked Brian.

"Yep."

"It appears that Mr. Gray *is* blackmailing Shawn Walker," said Sammy.

"I'm really confused now," said Phillips. "Detective Ann Flowers found out that Dr. Walker withdrew twenty-five thousand dollars from his bank at the time his son disappeared. If that was ransom money and Shawn didn't show up after it was paid, we thought he must be dead. Now you and this note say he's alive." Phillips drew his hands down over his face as if to wipe away the frustration. "It just doesn't make sense."

"Unless Shawn Walker faked his own kidnapping," said Sammy, wanting to cover all bases. He waited until that idea sank in. "He hated his father so he developed the kidnapping scheme. He collected the twenty-five thousand dollars and came up here."

"And," added Brian, "Les Gray knew that his best friend had faked his own kidnapping so he came up here to blackmail him."

"That still leaves two questions unanswered," said Sammy. "Why didn't his father report the kidnapping to the police? And, how did Les Gray find his friend so fast? Mr. Gray only arrived Monday with the other four from North Carolina."

"See what I mean?" said Phillips. "We still can't be sure whether Shawn Walker is alive or dead." He brushed his hand back over his sparse hair. "Oh, and I have another bit of information for you. According to Detective Flowers, Les Gray did some jail time." Before Sammy or Brian could ask, he added, "He robbed a store."

"That explains his criminal activity," said Brian. "The man's a crook."

Sammy stood and slipped two envelopes from his shirt pocket. "The answer to whether Mr. Walker is dead or alive might be right here." He handed two envelopes to Phillips.

"What do we have here?" asked the detective.

"Evidence, I hope," said Sammy. "If the fingerprints on either of the items in those envelopes match the prints on the watch crystal, then . . ."

"Are you saying that one of these prints belong to the real Shawn Walker?" asked Phillips.

Sammy shrugged. "Either Shawn Walker or the person who knows where he is."

Remembering Sammy's past track record for hunches, Phillips made arrangements for the fingerprints to be processed immediately. He also sent the note along with the envelopes. When that was taken care of, he glanced at his watch, looked at Sammy, and announced, "I'm going to be meeting with the people from North Carolina to compare notes in half an hour. If you want to stick around, you can join us in the conference room."

Sammy checked with Brian. "Sure, we'll stay." He shook hands with the actor and thanked him for a brilliant performance at Borders. "It takes a pro to pull off what you did. And I'm curious. Where is the gun you had under the table at the bookstore?"

The actor smiled. He raised his hand and extended his thumb and index finger. "Right here."

"Hmm," said Sammy, looking at the "hand-made" firearm. "Brian, that looks like your gun."

Brian raised his hand and extended his thumb and index finger. "Yep, they're the same," he said smiling. "Only his gun has more wrinkles than mine."

Everyone laughed.

Sammy was the first to turn serious. "Who were the two thugs you had standing on the other side of the window? Were they students of yours?" Sammy remembered that the retired actor was conducting acting classes.

"No, they were just two men looking over the book bargains on the table out there. One of the secrets of acting is to use what you have around you. Make your surroundings part of you. That's what I did. I developed fear in Les Gray by allowing those two men to become part of our little deception."

Sammy shook his head. "You had me believing it. We'll see you at the Barnes and Noble Bookstore Friday at five. You know what to do."

John Davenport lowered his brow and stabbed his finger into the air above him. In a deep voice and pronouncing each word distinctly, he said, "I'm an actor. Of course I know what to do." He picked up his discarded costume and headed for the door. "And now I must take leave of you peasants. I go to plan for my grand entrance and spectacular performance that I shall deliver on Friday."

"See, Brian, that's acting," said Phillips, remembering some of Brian's melodramatic renderings.

Brian was too embarrassed to say anything in front of the famous actor. Recalling the fabulous job the actor had done as "Henry Schnobel, the Third," Brian couldn't think of anything funny to say nor did he want to.

"Do you have a back way out of here?" asked Sammy. "We don't want the actor to be seen."

"Yeah," said Phillips, "I'll have Detective Wetzel show him the way."

After the actor had gone, Phillips played the tape made at Borders. Brian was interested in the part he had missed when he crept out to Les Gray's car.

After listening to the tape and adding praise for John Davenport's brilliant performance, Phillips led the way to the conference room. He poured himself a cup of coffee and apologized to the boys for not having sodas for them.

"Are you going to say anything to Les Gray or the others about what happened at Borders?" asked Sammy as they sat at the table.

"I'll only discuss what happened outside in Gray's car," said Phillips. "What happened inside the bookstore is your business." He smiled at Sammy. "Evidently you have a plan to disrupt Les Gray's blackmailing scheme."

"Yeah, and when you know, tell me," said Brian, remembering he was still mad at his buddy for not being told the full details of the plan.

Sammy nudged Brian. "We'll talk about it later at our brainstorming session." He was already formulating questions that he and Brian could use for ideas. Who was the masked man and what was he after? He was sure the masked man was not Shawn Walker. Why had the doctor withdrawn twenty-five thousand dollars from the bank soon after his son vanished? If it wasn't ransom money, what was it?"

Les Gray was the first of "The North Carolina Five" to show up. He appeared disheveled as he drifted into the room. He cast Brian a cold stare, causing the teenager to inch closer to Sammy. Gray grabbed a cup of coffee and sat at the end of the table, away from the amateur detectives.

"I heard you had an interesting time at the bookstore today," said Phillips.

"What do you mean?" asked Gray, his coffee making waves in the cup he was holding.

"I understand you were assaulted in your car by a man wearing a mask."

Gray focused on Brian. "Yeah, and by someone *not* wearing a mask. Why were you snooping on me? I'm one of the good guys here. I'm trying to find the truth about my friend, Shawn."

"From what Brian told us," said Phillips, "the masked man said *he* was Shawn. You knew Shawn better than anyone. Was the masked man your long lost friend?"

"No, he wasn't," replied Gray. "He disguised his voice, but he couldn't change his physical appearance. The man wasn't built like Shawn."

"But a person can change in twenty-two years," said Phillips. "I'm heavier now than I was twenty-two years ago."

Gray quickly sipped the coffee to lower the spill level. "All I'm saying is, it wasn't Shawn. I know it wasn't. He threatened me. It's someone who doesn't want Shawn found."

"Are you giving up the search for your friend?" asked Brian.

"I'm still thinking about it," said Gray.

Sammy was aware that someone had been standing by the opened doorway, listening. The super sleuth nudged Phillips and pointed to the shadow across the floor.

"Yes, who's there?" barked Phillips.

"Sorry I eavesdropped, but that's my job," said Dirk Evans, entering the room. "I heard Gray say he was threatened. I didn't want to interrupt so I stopped to listen. I, too, was given a warning. Can you believe it?"

"A masked man threatened you?" asked Brian.

Dirk chuckled. "No, I got a phone call in my room this afternoon. The voice said he was Shawn Walker. He said he wanted to be left alone, and that I was to go back to North Carolina immediately."

"And are you going?" asked Brian.

The investigator glanced at Gray. "No. And I don't have to think about it."

Fresh voices introduced three new arrivals to the room, Detective Ann Flowers, Leon Bradley, and Art Hansen. They all said their hellos then headed for the coffee.

"Have any of you received threats since you've been here in Lancaster?" asked Phillips.

"No," they each said.

"I want you to know that Les and Dirk here have been threatened," warned Phillips. "Be careful. Someone claiming to be Shawn Walker might try to intimidate you."

Detective Ann Flowers set her coffee and folders on the table opposite Phillips. "He better not try anything on me, or he'll be jailed in five minutes."

Leon Bradley, the retired cop, sat next to Ann. He was short, slim and bald, but his powerful voice let everyone know that an important person dwelled within his small frame. "I'll not completely retire until I find Walker," he bellowed. "No one is going to harass me to do otherwise." His voice echoed down the hall.

Art Hansen closed the door and sat next to Leon. The notebooks he carried were bulky. A writer's world was words, and he clutched his recent research as though it was the most precious thing in the world to him. He stacked the notebooks on the table and opened one, ready to take notes.

"Art," said Phillips, "I'm going to ask you to keep this quiet. I know you'll want the details for the story you're writing, but I don't want any information leaked to the public or the press right now. That goes for everybody here."

The corner of Detective Flowers' mouth curled at Phillips's remark. Her muscles tightened.

She didn't need to be reminded by a man about proper police procedures. She glanced at some notes then looked at Phillips. "With this recent development, are you still going with the notion that the twenty-five thousand dollars the doctor withdrew from his bank account was ransom money?"

"At this point, I don't know what to believe," said Phillips. "I don't know if Walker is dead or alive. But let's keep all options open. Yesterday, a young girl delivered a note to the Bird-in-Hand Country Store. The typed note said he didn't want to be found. It was signed Shawn Walker."

Everyone gasped.

"But you just said . . ."

"Which at this point doesn't mean anything," continued Phillips. "Anyone could have sent the note. The girl vanished after she delivered the message."

"What exactly did the note say?" asked the writer. "May I see it?"

Phillips gave Sammy a quick glance and said, "The note is being examined at the lab for prints and such. But it stated that he wanted Sammy and Brian to do what they could to help keep his life private." Phillips didn't mention the part that said Les Gray was blackmailing Walker. He shrugged and continued. "Evidently, Mr. Walker wants to be left alone."

Sammy watched Les Gray's reactions throughout the discussion. After the meeting broke up, Sammy asked Phillips if he could do a background check on Les Gray. He needed to know more about this blackmailer. The young detective felt strongly that Shawn Walker had written the note. He was almost certain that Les Gray was blackmailing Walker. What he couldn't understand was the masked man. What was his game? Who would he assault next?

CHAPTER ELEVEN

Ten minutes after the meeting was over at the police station, a car pulled in at the Bird-in-Hand Family Inn. The driver reached into the glove compartment and withdrew a handful of black knit material.

A ski mask.

The mask was shoved under the belt. But who would notice with the excitement of the tourists and passing cars and Amish buggies. "The Mask" traveled on foot the half mile from the inn, past the farmer's market to the post office. From there in the shadows, the bare face could see down, across the street to the Wilsons' house and their store. As the sun took its last peek at Amish farmland, the face waited for the call of the mask.

The ceiling lay heavy over Brian as he reclined on the bed. He was sifting through the events of the last couple of days. Sammy stood by the bedroom window, peering into the shadows across the street. When he was satisfied no one was lurking there, he returned to his desk.

They had just returned from the police station where the others had reported on their search efforts to find Walker. Other than the intrusion of the masked man and his demands, nothing worthy of mention emerged from their reports. "The North Carolina Five" were not told what had occurred inside the bookstore. And Les Gray had no reason to mention his bout with the old man.

"If Shawn Walker is alive," said Brian, "then he sealed his watch into the tin box and placed it behind the stone. He was trying to get rid of it. Why?"

Sammy went to his desk, sat, and leaned toward Brian. "Brian, what's in your tin box that you want to hide?"

Brian lifted his head. "What do you mean? I don't have a tin box."

"We all have a tin box that we carry with us all the time."

"We do?"

"It's called the subconscious. That's where we store all our experiences."

Brian's head flopped back on the bed. "If this is one of your metaphors, I don't want to hear it."

"Brian, think about it. Can you imagine what it would be like if everything you ever experienced remained in your conscious mind? That you were always aware of all the things that ever happened to you."

"My conscious mind would be so cluttered, I wouldn't be able to think straight," said Brian, showing more interest.

"Correct," said Sammy. "Isn't it great that we can store all that information into the subconscious to save for us?"

"Yeah," said Brian, "and it saves it until we need it. But there's some stuff there I'd rather not save."

"Oh? What's that?" asked Sammy.

"I don't want to say. It's too personal."

"That bad, huh?" said Sammy, smiling. "Well, I have something I'd like to get rid of in my tin box. The guilt of having taken a book in a store without paying for it."

Brian sat up. "You! You stole a book?"

"I'll never forget it. I was almost nine years old. My mother wouldn't buy the book for me so I took it. I wanted to read it so badly."

"Yeah? Do you remember what book it was?" asked Brian.

"Oh, yes," said Sammy. He stood and went to his wall-to-wall bookcase. "My subconscious won't let me forget it." He pulled the book from a lower shelf and held it for Brian to see. "It's Ray Bradbury's *Something Wicked This Way Comes*."

Brian scratched the back of his neck. "That's the book you stole?"

"Well, no, this isn't the same book. The reason my mother wouldn't buy the book for me was she had already purchased the book—for my birthday."

"So now you have two of the same book," said Brian.

"No. The book I stole I took back to the store and replaced it on the shelf."

"So that erased it. Why do you feel guilty? You put it back," said Brian.

"That doesn't erase the fact that I took the book in the first place."

"Sure it does. You put it back."

"I'm afraid not," said Sammy. "The damage had already been done."

"What damage?" asked Brian.

"Brian, if I hammer a nail into the top of this oak desk, is that bad?"

"It's not good," replied Brian.

"Now, if I pull the nail out again, would I be undoing what I had done?"

"No, there's still a hole in the desk."

"Exactly," said Sammy. "The damage remains."

"Oh, I get it. Every time we do something bad, it's like driving a nail into a piece of wood. Even though we're sorry and pull the nail out, the hole remains."

"Now," said Sammy as he replaced the book on the shelf, "do you want to tell me what you have hidden away in your tin box?"

Brian took a deep breath. "I took a candy bar from a drug store when I was eight." He waited for his friend to say something. When he didn't, Brian continued. "It was a dumb thing to do. I'll never forget it."

"That's my point," said Sammy. "Shawn Walker tried to make his past go away by hiding it behind a stone in the wall. If he walked away twenty-two years ago, he broke no laws. But the damage is there. The memory lingers on."

"And now he's being blackmailed," said Brian.

Sammy wondered over to the window. The flow of tourists and locals was thinning out. Some of the shops had closed for the night. But in the darkness between the house and the antique shop, something moved.

The mysterious dark shadow was back!

Sammy casually walked away from the window but then dashed past Brian, pulling him from the bed. "Come on, there's someone watching from across the street."

Sammy shouted directions to Brian as they hurried down the stairs. "You go out through the back of the house and around to your right. I'll go to the left to the side road. We'll meet across the street at the antique shop."

When Sammy arrived out front, he joined some tourists as they crossed the street. He pretended to enter the antique shop. At the last minute he darted to his left to confront the stalker.

Reflected light filtered into the narrow area and was enough for the teenager to see the figure.

The man was as scared as Sammy. He held his arms up in front to protect himself. "Hey, wait a minute! It's me!" yelled Art Hansen.

"What are you doing here?" asked Sammy.

Brian came running up with a yellow plastic bat in his hand. "Stand back. I'll hit him if he tries anything."

Sammy grabbed the bat and lowered it. "It's okay, Brian. It's Art Hansen, the writer."

Brian was disappointed he didn't get to swing the bat and bring another criminal to justice. "Why are you spying on us?" he asked.

"I wasn't spying on you." He pointed to the shop next to Sammy's house. "I was watching your parents' store."

"You were here last night, too. Why?" asked Sammy.

"Hey, I'm a writer, and you boys are where the action is. Why should I be somewhere else? You remember at the police station earlier, Detective Phillips said that a girl delivered that note to your parents' store. Well, I thought she might come back. Or, better still, that Shawn Walker would come and pay you a visit."

Brian created his secret agent pose. "So you're standing out here waiting for that to happen. Is that your story, Mr. Hansen? Well I don't buy it." Brian raised the flimsy bat, getting ready to hit a homer.

"A plastic bat?" said Sammy. "Where's the little plastic ball that goes with it?"

"Okay," said Brian, "so I tripped over the bat, running across the back yard. It was there so I grabbed it."

"I don't think Mr. Hansen is going to attack us with his notebook," said Sammy. He turned back to the writer. "Come up to my room, we'll talk about it there."

"So you thought that by staking out our place, you might run into Shawn Walker," said Sammy after everyone had settled down in the bedroom.

The writer sat on the rocker which didn't endear him to Brian. Art rubbed his palms nervously over the wooden arms. At the moment, he was showing his sixty-some years. "I've done worse than this in my quest for a story."

"So have we," said Sammy. "Remember, Brian, in the Doom Buggy case, we staked out the welding shop? We sat by the creek, pretending to fish." Sammy was trying to get Brian to relax a little.

"Yeah, Joyce was with us," said Brian with a bite to his words. He peered at Art Hansen sitting in the rocking chair. He didn't like the idea of a "foreigner" from North Carolina coming up here spying on them and then taking over Joyce's rocker. Brian didn't buy the reason for Art Hansen's behavior.

Sammy had no reason to distrust the writer. He was sincere enough. "How's the story coming along?" asked Sammy.

"Okay, I guess," said Hansen. "I'd like to see some action to bring the story to a close. What I'm saying is, I'd like to see an ending of this story."

"That's right. This story started twenty-two years ago," said Sammy.

Art Hansen shifted the notebook on his lap. "I was in my early forties, a reporter, and I hadn't written that big story yet. The missing college student was going to be my big break. It had potential for a great story. But then nothing materialized for twenty-two years—until you boys found the box. And now my hopes are high again." Art Hansen sighed. "All we need is the truth about Shawn Walker."

"Ah," said Sammy, "there's the title for your book—*The Truth About Shawn Walker.*"

The writer lifted his eyebrows. "Not bad. Maybe I'll use it."

"It must be tough trying to make a living when you're a writer," said Brian.

"It's not so bad. I'm what you call a stringer. When I'm not working on a book, I work part-time as a free-lance news correspondent for various newspapers and magazines."

"Are you married?" asked Sammy.

"Yes, I have a wife, Jane, and five children."

Sammy felt this man needed some positive news, some hope. "I have reason to believe that a meeting will take place at Barnes and Noble Friday at five o'clock in the afternoon. That encounter should provide the evidence we need to finally answer two questions. Where is Shawn Walker? And, is he dead or alive?"

Art's face went blank. His mouth opened. Finally he spoke. "How do you know that?"

"Let's just say it has to do with the note delivered by the girl," answered Sammy.

Satisfied with the explanation coming from the young detective, Art Hansen quickly entered that information into his notebook.

After ten more minutes of speculating as to the motivation and identity of the masked man, Art Hansen left.

When Sammy returned from showing the writer to the door, Brian asked, "Why did you tell him about Barnes and Noble on Friday?"

Sammy shrugged. "I don't know. Maybe I wanted to give him hope, to see the light at the end of the tunnel."

"Boy, I don't even see the tunnel," said Brian. "Now, what's behind the story that John Davenport told Les Gray—about buying land in Lancaster County?"

"Okay, here it is," said Sammy. "Les Gray has something on Shawn Walker. If we do anything to stop the blackmail, Les Gray will know that Mr. Walker told us. He will then expose the damaging information he has about him. My plan involves letting Les Gray collect the blackmail money. Then we will collect it back from him."

"But he's only giving 'Henry Schnobel, the Third,' twenty-five thousand. That's half of the fifty thousand. How are we getting back the other twenty-five—steal it?"

Sammy grinned. "We're not going to steal it. We're going to have Les Gray hand it over to us."

Brian slid off the bed. "Hey, I get it now. That's what the land investment deal is all about. You had John Davenport mention the investment deal to suck Les Gray into your con game."

"Right," said Sammy.

"But John Davenport told him that they didn't need more investors. They already had eight people, each putting fifty thousand dollars into the deal."

"Would it surprise you, Brian, to learn that at the last minute, Les Gray will be permitted to invest in the land deal?"

"So John Davenport, playing the part of Henry Schnobel, the Third, will mention that one of the investors is short twenty-five thousand dollars. Now Les Gray will be anxious to invest his twenty-five thousand dollars, which he will never see again. And Shawn Walker will get back his fifty thousand dollars."

"If the plan works," added Sammy. "Only if the plan works."

Some disturbing noise was coming from outside. The boys rushed to the front window. Whatever was creating the noise, it was not coming from in front of the house. They went from the bedroom, through the hall, to the window overlooking the small parking area in front of his parents' shop. What they saw caused the super sleuths to race down the steps and out of the house.

Several people were gathered around Art Hansen. A man, breathing heavily, came running to join the crowd. "I chased him up the street but he disappeared somewhere. I couldn't find him."

"What happened?" asked Sammy, working his way closer to Art Hansen.

"It was the masked man again," said Hansen. "I came out here, opened the door of my car and got in. Then this guy wearing a ski mask kept me from closing the door. He said I should go home and forget about Shawn Walker and my story."

"Yeah, I was at my car," said the bystander who was still trying to catch his breath. "I saw the man wearing a mask run away. I thought it was a mugging so I ran after the guy. But he disappeared up the street."

"Are you hurt?" asked Brian.

"Not physically—just mentally," answered Hansen. "The masked man took my notes and the research I did today. He said that if I quit searching for Walker, I'd get my written material back."

"At least you're all right," said Sammy. "You better report this to Detective Phillips." Sammy turned and walked to the front edge of the parking area and glanced east, the direction the masked man had fled.

Brian followed. "What's up? What are you thinking?"

Sammy pointed. "Our mystery man ran in that direction."

"So?" said Brian.

"The Bird-in-Hand Family Inn is one-half mile up the road. That's where our five visitors are staying."

"Yeah," said Brian, "and you know what I'm thinking? Three of 'The North Carolina Five' have received threats. If we wait until one more gets a visit from the man in the mask, the one who's left will have to be our man."

"Or woman," said Sammy, thinking of Detective Ann Flowers.

CHAPTER TWELVE

The next day, Thursday, the principal escorted the amateur detectives to the Brownstown Elementary School. Their presentation followed the pattern of their first assembly program. The students and teachers alike were excited to hear of the boys' adventures and the finding of the tin box. The boys were then scheduled to appear at the Fritz Elementary School the next Monday and the Leola Elementary School on Wednesday.

Later after school, Sammy received a call from Detective Phillips. It was both good news and bad news. The good news was that the fingerprints from one sample Sammy had given to Phillips matched the prints on the watch crystal. The bad news was that Leon Bradley, the retired cop, had been badly beaten and was in the hospital. The ski mask had struck again!

It was hard for Brian to concentrate on his homework. Sometimes Sammy and he did their schoolwork together in Sammy's room. Brian would then go home, wait around for supper, then return at seven for their brainstorming session. But Brian couldn't wait for later to discuss the new turn of events.

He read the same page over and over and finally gave up. He pushed his schoolbook aside, slid off the bed, and sat on the floor. Resting his head back against the bed, he looked up at Sammy. "With Leon Bradley in the hospital, that leaves only one left—Detective Flowers. So she's the masked man . . . er, masked woman. Right, Sammy?"

Sammy frowned as he peered over his oak desk. "Brian, can't you let it go until later? We both have some other learning to do."

"Who are you kidding? You already know all that stuff. You know you're going to get A's on all your tests. You know everything."

"Brian, if I get A's it's because I care about myself. I want to learn. I listen in class and think about what I'm learning. I read and think about what I'm reading. If I already knew everything, I wouldn't have to do all of that. All I'd have to do was to show up and take the test."

"But I do all of that and I don't get A's."

"Brian, *doing* it doesn't make you learn it. *Feeling it* makes you learn it. Your whole self has to become part of the learning process."

"Well, right now I have a *feeling* that Detective Flowers is our man."

Sammy took a deep breath and resigned himself to the fact that Brian was not going to give up. "She may be the person behind the mask, but what reason would she have for not wanting Shawn Walker found?"

Brian thought about that for a few seconds and then grinned. "If someone other than the North Carolina police found Mr. Walker, wouldn't that make their police department look bad?"

"So you're saying Detective Ann Flowers wants to be the person who finds Shawn Walker. That's pretty good, Brian."

"Sure, I *felt it.*"

Placing a marker in his book and laying his pencil aside, Sammy gave full attention to Brian. "But why would she beat up on Leon Bradley? Even if he is retired, he still represents their police department."

Brian kept rolling. He realized their brainstorming had started early. "Maybe if Mr. Walker is found, Mr. Bradley will want to take the credit for it."

Sammy agreed. "Detective Flowers does seem to be self-centered. She gives me the impression she wants to do things her way."

"Right," said Brian. "And her way is to get everybody else out of the way."

Sammy thought of the warning note he had found on the floor at the station. It had come from one of the five. Had Detective Ann Flowers written it? The teenager thought of the attacks by the person wearing the ski mask. Would he and Brian be next? First it was Les Gray, who had been a good friend of the missing man. He was threatened in his car. Then Dirk Evans, the investigator, had received a threatening phone call. Art Hansen, the writer, was assaulted in his car and had his notes taken. Leon Bradley, retired cop, was attacked physically. "Hey, wait a minute," said Sammy as he jumped up from his desk.

"What's wrong?" asked Brian, standing.

"You go back to doing your homework. I'm going up to the Bird-in-Hand Family Inn. I want to check on something. I'll be right back."

Brian frowned. "I'll wait here and think about tomorrow."

"Brian, let me ask you one question," said Sammy as he stood at the door.

"And what's that?" asked Brian.

"Why would you want to keep yourself from learning? Don't you like yourself? Aren't you worth it?" Sammy didn't wait for an answer.

"That's three questions," Brian shouted as his friend descended the stairway. When Brian heard the front door close, he went to the window and watched as Sammy mounted his bike and headed up the street. Brian turned toward the bed and his books. Sure, I like myself, he thought. No one likes me more than me. He stood straight and tall and thought of himself as secret agent, double-oh-seven and a half. Now, did he want to be a dumb agent or a smart agent? The decision was his. He glanced at his schoolbooks. He smiled, mounted the bed, and quickly found the page to continue his assignment.

When Sammy returned forty-five minutes later, he found Brian absorbed in his social studies.

"Hey, Sammy, this trench warfare is neat but scary. Did you know that in the trenches, the soldiers had to fight off rats as large as cats? The rats were after the food, I guess. And the lice . . ."

Sammy sat and listened to his buddy rattle off the adventures and hardships endured by the soldiers. Most of the horrors were told in letters written in the trenches and mailed back to the comforts of home.

"Brian, now you're feeling it," said Sammy. "Isn't it great that we can learn about war without having to be in it?"

"Speaking of war," said Brian, closing his book, "we have to discuss how we're going to bunker in at Barnes and Noble tomorrow after school."

Sammy dragged two large plastic bags from behind his desk. "We're not going to Barnes and Noble tomorrow."

Brian's mouth dropped. He jumped up from the bed. "What do you mean, we're not going?" asked Brian.

Sammy hurled a filled bag at his friend, causing Brian to fall back on the bed. "Sammy and Brian aren't going, but Billy and Burt are."

CHAPTER THIRTEEN

T he two fifteen-year-old boys who entered Barnes and Noble at 4:45 did not resemble Sammy and Brian. The tall boy had his straight, dark hair combed down to his bushy eyebrows and blue eyes. His head was topped with an Orioles baseball cap. His knit shirt collar was turned up. Marks on his face showed the results of a hard life.

The short teenager wore plastic-rimmed glasses. His brown, wavy hair was parted in the middle with some stragglers standing up. His puffed-out cheeks and the extra weight around his middle gave evidence that he ate more than three meals a day. If you lifted the adhesive tape along his left eye, you'd find no injury.

The amateur detectives were in disguise—incognito.

It was neat, pretending to be someone else. Sammy headed straight for the magazine racks. Brian waddled behind. They positioned themselves on a bench between two bookracks. From there they had a clear view of the café area.

Several tables were occupied. Two young women were relaxing as they sipped Starbucks coffee. A man was taking notes from a paperback book. Another table contained an open book and papers waiting for the user to return.

On a bench outside the café railing, a familiar figure hunched over a newspaper. The boys couldn't mistake the salt and pepper hair and large nose. It was the investigator, Dirk Evans.

Brian pushed the glasses higher on his nose and nudged Sammy. "Hey, what's he doing here?"

"I'm wondering the same thing," said Sammy. "He could wreck our plans."

Brian glanced around and then checked his watch. "Les Gray should be here soon. If they recognize each other, that's bad news," he said.

"We have someone else to contend with," said Sammy as he brushed hair away from his eyes. "Look who's over there behind the checkout counter."

Brian shifted his extra bulk and stared. "Art Hansen. Looks like he's interviewing the sales clerk."

"Yeah, but he's keeping his eyes on the café," said Sammy.

"What did you expect?" asked Brian. "You told him about the meeting. Do you think he'll interfere with your plan?"

"No, he's no threat," said Sammy. "He's here to write the story. He doesn't want to become part of it. He'll be content to watch it develop, and stay out of the way."

At that moment a casually dressed man, carrying a cloth bag, walked past the super sleuths. He picked out a magazine and went into the café. Les Gray had gone right by the boys and had not recognized them.

"Oh, there's Mr. Gray," said Brian. He stared at Dirk Evans to see his reaction to Gray's appearance. The investigator immediately zeroed in on Gray. Is that why Dirk Evans is here? wondered Brian. Was he here to spy on Mr. Gray? Did he suspect that Gray was blackmailing Shawn Walker?

The dialog cloud that hovered above Sammy's head contained one question—Would anyone or anything disrupt his plan?

Dirk Evans turned his back to the railing as Gray bought coffee and selected a table near the back of the café. Dirk took side glances, watching Gray carefully positioning a small duffel bag between his feet under the table. Gray then opened the magazine and sipped at the hot coffee.

The veteran actor made his entrance on cue. His earthy attire brought stares from the customers in the bookstore. A girl at the checkout counter wondered if he had left his tractor parked outside. A young boy envisioned him as an old prospector panning for gold and was now bringing his nuggets into the big city to spend.

The old man ambled his way to the café. He raised his hat, affording himself a better view of the area. When he spotted Les Gray, he made a beeline for his table.

Gray peeked over the magazine to identify the man who had suddenly joined him. "You're early."

The stern expression on the hairy face told Gray that Henry Schnobel, the Third, was in no mood for social chitchat. This was a business transaction, plain and simple. Get it over with and each will go on his way.

"Well, I'm waiting for it," said the old man.

Following the sound of a zipper, a bulging plastic bag appeared quickly from under the table. "Here. Twenty-five thousand. Take it."

The old man opened the bag. He didn't want to wait until later to find out that the bag contained cut paper. He saw green. It was money. Big bills. "Okay, partner, our transaction is done," squeaked the old man. "I thank you for your honest effort, and should I ever again need a partner—"

Gray clutched the old man's arm before he had a chance rise. "How are things going with your land investment deal?" he asked.

"Why do you care?" asked the old timer. "You're going to scoot back to North Carolina."

"How do you know that?" snapped Gray.

"Your roots are there. You can't grow without roots," said the old man.

Gray raised an eyebrow. "I can grow anywhere if I have enough money for fertilizer."

"You have twenty-five thousand. Don't be greedy," said the old man.

"I'll ask you one more time," said Gray. "Are you sure I can't invest in your land deal?"

"No way," answered the old timer. "It's locked up tight."

"Oh, yeah? Well, what happens if GMU Tri-Cepters receives a letter that exposes your scheme to exploit inside information?"

The old man's voice ripped into a strained muffled threat. "Don't you even think of anything like that or you're history."

Les Gray looked around, expecting to see the old man's thugs come charging toward him. When he didn't, he leaned closer. "Look, we're two of a kind. We'd make a great pair. I have some great ideas for us to make big money."

The old man grinned. "The fifty thousand you got from Shawn Walker. You call that big money?" He patted the bag sitting on the table. "And I got half of that. Some big hustler you are."

The silence and the deflated look from Les Gray told John Davenport, the actor, that now was the time. "Okay, I'll tell you what I'll do. Since I can't be sure if and when you might send that letter to GMU Tri-Cepters, I'll let you invest. Instead of my going to the bank to cash in some bonds, I'll put your money with mine to make the fifty thousand I need for my share."

Gray's eyes lit up. "Then we'll split the two hundred thousand dollars we get when GMU Tri-Cepters buys the land."

"Right," said the old man. "One hundred thousand each."

Gray reached under the table then stopped. He looked at the man he had just met three days ago. "How do I know I'll ever see you again after I give you this money?"

The actor sat back and adjusted his hat on his head. "Look, you're not helping matters, *partner*. If I wanted to rip you off, I would produce my gun and take all your money right now. Am I doing that?"

Before Gray could answer, someone walked up to the table.

"Hey, Henry, how are you doing?" came a voice from behind. The young man was dressed in a business suit like thousands of others who worked in the business world.

The old geezer's face grimaced as he reluctantly stood, forced a smile, and shook hands. "David, what are you doing these days?"

"Oh, investing here, investing there. And you? I heard you might be into something big right now."

"Yeah, there's something on the burner," replied the old man.

David shook his head. "I never question how or where you do it, but you always come through. Do you have anything open right now? I have some cash I can move in your direction."

"No, sorry," said the old man. He sat and faced Gray to let David know that their conversation was over.

"Well, if anything comes up, let me know," said the young man. He turned and walked away.

"Sorry about that," said the old man. "The guy's a loser. But it doesn't hurt to be associated with socially accepted business people."

Without wasting time, Gray kicked the duffel bag around the table legs so it ended up beside the old man's chair. "There. Now how do we keep in touch?"

The actor slipped a napkin in front of Gray. "Give me your phone number in North Carolina where I can reach you. I'll call you in two months. I can either send you the money, or we can set up a place to meet."

While Gray wrote the number, the actor placed his bag of money next to the other money already in the cloth bag. He gave a sigh of relief as he closed the zipper over Shawn Walker's fifty thousand dollars.

Sammy and Brian watched as the actor wiped his nose with his red and blue bandanna. It was the signal that the plan had worked. Shawn Walker's money was now in the actor's possession.

Sammy and Brian had recognized the young man in the business suit who had helped jump-start the con game. He was a student from John Davenport's acting class.

Dirk Evans hadn't moved. He seemed content to just sit there and watch the drama unfold. He had witnessed the passing of the duffel bag. That disturbed Sammy. But now what? Did Dirk Evans think that the old man was Shawn Walker in disguise and that Gray had passed him money? That thought gave Sammy a great idea.

"Well, Sammy and Brian," said a whispered voice from beside the bookrack.

The boys looked up at the massive figure with the formidable eyes. "That was quite a show your actor friend put on," said Detective Ben Phillips. "I couldn't hear everything, but I saw the money being passed."

"I wondered where you were hiding," said Sammy.

Brian rubbed his padded stomach and adjusted his glasses. "How did you recognize us?" he asked in a voice that had to work its way through cotton padded cheeks.

"Well, chubby, don't forget. I'm a trained professional. My x-ray eyes can—"

"Stop it, please," said Sammy to Phillips. "You're starting to sound like Brian. And one of him is enough." Sammy turned serious. "Did you see Dirk Evans over there?"

"Yeah, and Art Hansen. What are they doing here?" asked Phillips. "Are they part of your plan, too?"

"No," said Sammy. "And it wouldn't surprise

me to find Detective Ann Flowers hiding around here somewhere."

Detective Phillips smiled. "Later, I'm having my last meeting with our five visitors from North Carolina before they go home tomorrow. If you want to bring charges against any one of them, show up at seven o'clock."

"Brian and I will be there." Sammy's eyes shifted to the movement from the table. The actor and Les Gray were leaving.

"They're going," said Brian. "What do we do now?"

Sammy hurriedly printed something in his notebook, tore a page loose, and forced it into Brian's hand. "Here, take this quickly and give it to Dirk Evans. Tell him a man told you to deliver it. Then head outside. I'll meet you around to the left of the building."

Brian knew better then to ask questions. Instead he scampered off in Dirk's direction, repeating Sammy's directions to himself.

"What's the message?" asked Detective Phillips.

"Meet me in the music section. And I signed it Shawn Walker. I don't want Mr. Evans to follow the actor. We can't afford for him to learn about the blackmail and to find out that this was a setup."

Phillips smiled. "I think I better hurry and strike up a conversation with Art Hansen. We can't have him get too nosy either."

"Yeah, thanks," said Sammy. "And later, have your handcuffs ready. There will be charges brought."

"You know who the masked man is?" asked Phillips.

"Yes, and I know why."

CHAPTER FOURTEEN

T he person being catered to was Leon Bradley. His release from the hospital had come with a warning to stay off his feet and rest. Ann Flowers poured an extra cup of coffee and placed it in front of the recovering patient. Art was getting personal details of the assault, while Dirk shoved a stool under Leon's legs.

Dirk was hurting from falling for a setup that kept him from trailing the old man. He had waited fifteen minutes in the music department and no one had shown up.

Several small bandages still covered Leon's swollen face. His arm was in a sling. The masked man tried to make the point that retirement meant retirement. Leon was to get off the case and stay off.

Les Gray paid no attention to Leon Bradley or the others. He isolated himself in the corner of the conference room and thought of the hundred thousand dollars he would be receiving in two months. He scowled at Sammy and Brian as they entered the room with Detective Phillips.

Phillips was the first to speak. "You all came up here to Lancaster in response to the contents of the tin box," said Phillips. "You wanted to know whether Shawn Walker was dead or still alive. Did he run away? Did he have an accident? Was he abducted? While we don't know the answers to all those questions, we do know this. Shawn Walker is alive."

That got everyone's attention, especially Les Gray's. The condition of the fifty-thousand-dollar blackmail payoff to him was that Shawn Walker's identity was not to be revealed. Les moved his chair closer to the table.

"And we have one person to thank for finding Shawn Walker for us," said Sammy.

"And who is that?" asked Ann Flowers.

"Les Gray," said Sammy as he went and stood by him. "Mr. Gray had a meeting with Shawn Walker today at Barnes and Noble bookstore. Didn't you, Mr. Gray?" The young detective patted Gray on the back, each time inserting pressure with his index finger. "Isn't that right? You met with Shawn Walker and he was disguised as an old man."

Les was startled at the misleading bit of information that Sammy had added to the facts. He didn't understand where this was going, but he went along with Sammy's statement. "Yes, that's correct," said Gray.

Sammy continued. "Mr. Evans and Art Hansen, I believe you can verify that because you were there."

Dirk was reluctant to answer, but after a few seconds, he said, "Yeah, I saw Les talking to the old man, or at least I thought he was an old man. I didn't know at the time that it was Shawn Walker."

"Yeah, I saw Les talking to an old man," said Hansen, "but I had no idea it was Walker wearing a disguise. How do you know it was really him?"

"Only one person here is qualified to identify Walker. That's his boyhood, best friend. Mr. Gray knew Shawn Walker better than his own parents."

Since nothing incriminating was being said about him, Les was willing to be in the spotlight. "I knew something about Shawn that nobody else knew," said Gray proudly. "I followed that lead and I found him."

Art Hansen and Dirk Evans had seen the old man leave the bookstore carrying a duffel bag. Knowing this, Sammy added, "And in Barnes and Noble you gave him some personal things you brought from North Carolina. Right, Mr. Gray," said Sammy applying go-along-with-it pressure to his back.

"That's right. He made me promise not to tell anyone who or where he is. That's why I didn't report to you that I found him. He has established a new life. He is happy and wishes to remain anonymous." Les sat back and relaxed. He was pleased with his little speech.

Phillips continued. "We will honor Shawn Walker's wishes. He has broken no laws. He wanted to break away from his early life, which he had a right to do. He came up here, established a new identity, and is living a worthwhile life. He just wants to be left alone."

Ann Flowers shook her head. "What about the two million dollars that's his in a trust fund? Doesn't he want it?"

Everyone looked at Les Gray.

He shrugged. "I guess not."

"We have one more problem to dispose of before you go back to North Carolina," said Detective Phillips. "Who's the person behind the mask? Who wanted you to stop investigating this case by using threats and bodily harm?"

"Do you know who attacked me?" asked Leon. "Who was it?"

Sammy walked around the table and stopped at Art Hansen. "Only one person here wanted Shawn Walker *not* to be found. Was it Art Hansen? No, he wanted Mr. Walker found so he would finally have an ending to his story." Sammy moved to Leon Bradley. "Mr. Bradley wanted Mr. Walker found so he could finally retire."

Detective Flowers squirmed in her chair as Sammy approached. She didn't need a male to tell her anything.

"Detective Flowers wanted to find him so she could get credit for solving the case. Which is what any hard-working detective would want. But would that be enough reason to wear a mask and harass others? I don't think so."

Sammy moved to Les Gray. "Did Mr. Gray want to find his long lost friend? Yes, he did." Sammy didn't mention the reason was to blackmail him. "And that leaves just one more person. Investigator, Dirk Evans."

"It wasn't me. I wanted him found. Did you forget I was threatened like the rest of them?"

"I don't think so," said Sammy. "We only have your word for it. You said you received the threat by a phone call to your room in the afternoon. I checked with the Bird-in-Hand Family Inn. You received no phone calls that afternoon."

"Maybe I got the days mixed up."

"I'm sorry, but the records show you had no incoming calls to your room since you've been here. You only used your phone to call out."

"But why wouldn't I want Walker found? I promised his father as he was dying that I would never give up my search for his son."

"I can believe that, Mr. Evans," said Sammy. "It's been twenty-two years and you're still looking. And as long as he's not found, as long as he doesn't return and collect his inheritance, you and your foundation continue to receive the interest from the trust fund. How much do you receive every year, Mr. Evans? What is the interest earned on two million dollars? I figured you get about two hundred thousand a year."

Dirk Evans looked at the others in the room. They believed what Sammy was saying. There was anger in Leon's eyes. Detective Flowers's face was stern, showing disgust for the man. Art was writing, not missing a fact or description. Les Gray was visualizing Dirk in his car wearing the mask, remembering the words that were said.

"You can't prove a thing," said Dirk. He stood and started to leave.

Sammy moved closer. "Why were you at Barnes and Noble today, watching Les Gray meet with the old man?"

Dirk stopped. "You forget, I'm investigating Walker's disappearance. I had a reason to be there."

"But you weren't trailing Mr. Gray. You were there before he arrived. How did you know about the meeting?"

"I . . . ah . . ."

"You knew because you read about the meeting in the notes you stole from Art Hansen. He was the only person we told about the meeting, and that information was part of his notes."

"Where are my notes? I want them back," said the writer.

Detective Phillips approached Dirk Evans. "When we search your car and your room at the inn, I think we'll recover the missing notes and the ski mask. You're under arrest, Dirk Evans, for terroristic threats and assault."

Dirk froze. He didn't know what to say. His face was pale. He had been caught.

As Detective Phillips was about to leave the room with his prisoner, he turned and faced the others. "As far as I'm concerned, this case is closed."

———————————————

Everything was back to normal by Monday. The sky was clear and blue, predicting a fine day. Four of "The North Carolina Five" had returned home. Dirk Evans hadn't put up bail money so he remained in jail until his court appearance before a judge.

The news media had mentioned the latest developments in the case. The masked man had been unmasked by Sammy Wilson and Brian Helm. However, no mention was made of the blackmail or what had transpired inside the bookshop.

The police were under no obligation to report to the media that Shawn Walker had been found. Mr. Walker's privacy would remain intact. Detective Ben Phillips had closed the case.

The Fritz Elementary School was buzzing with excitement as the super sleuths arrived for the special program. Mr. Baksa, the high school principal, introduced the boys, then stood back to let the amateur detectives tell their story.

Brian spoke first, describing some of their early cases. Then Sammy told how the tin box was discovered buried behind the stone wall *in the cellar*. Since the case was closed, the location of the buried box could now be revealed.

"And I have a surprise for you," said Sammy. He withdrew an object from a paper bag and held it high. "This is the actual tin box that we found."

Brian gave a little cough.

"The tin box that *Brian* found," said Sammy. "And inside is . . ." He took out the watch and the news article.

"Ahs" and "ohs" came from the audience as Sammy and Brian proceeded to walk around the all-purpose room, showing the items up close. Brian pointed out the deterioration of the box from being buried twenty-two years. Sammy showed the inscription on the back of the watch.

The program came to a close with questions and comments.

"Brian, were you scared when you were in the car with the masked man?"

The aspiring amateur detective stood tall and in a deep voice said, "You get used to fear. That's when you do your best work." Brian squared his shoulders. "My innate ability allowed me to conceal myself on the floor of the car so that I could gather vital information that would help crack this case."

"But they found you."

Before Brian could continue, Sammy jumped in. "Yes, we all get scared at times like that." Sammy quickly pointed to another upheld hand.

"You didn't find the missing man. What happened to him?" asked a fifth-grade girl.

Sammy didn't want to reveal information that might infringe on Shawn Walker's right of privacy. "I have a feeling that Mr. Walker is alive. He buried this tin with his watch and the article about his past. He probably wanted to forget that part of his life." Sammy pointed to the students. "Were there ever times when something happened to you and you felt like running away? Or wished it never happened?"

"Yeah, I did run away," shouted a boy. "My dad and mom—"

"That's okay, Kevin," said his teacher. "He gets the idea."

"I don't think Mr. Walker wants to be found," continued Sammy. "He enjoys being who he is and doesn't want to be reminded of his past."

A sixth-grade boy raised his hand. "The television said the masked man was getting some of Mr. Walker's money down in North Carolina. Why doesn't Mr. Walker go down and get his money?"

"It's possible that he didn't know that his father left him money," said Sammy. "But now that it's been in the news, maybe he will."

More questions were asked, the program ended, and the three headed back to the high school.

Brian sat in the back of the car checking out the lay of the land. A red car was following them. Brian frowned as he watched from the back window. Could it be another evildoer trailing the famous secret agent, Brian Helm? he wondered.

He watched as the red car zoomed by them. He shrugged. It must be a terrible burden, he thought, to own a red car, knowing that you always had to drive fast and pass all the other cars in front of you.

Sammy sat in the front seat. The tin box rested on his lap. He bit his lip, took a deep breath, and raised the box in his left hand. "Here, I believe this box belongs to you."

Mr. Baksa looked straight ahead and said nothing. He couldn't speak. Tears formed. The car slowed down, and he pulled over to the side of the road and stopped. The car was quiet. No one said a thing, but the words, "I believe this box belongs to you," lingered. Brian was shocked into silence.

Finally the principal looked at the box and then at Sammy. "How did you know?"

Sammy spoke softly. "The first time you called Brian and me to your office, you talked about us finding this box. You asked what we were doing in the cellar. The police hadn't released the information as to exactly where the tin box was found, remember?"

The principal nodded.

Sammy continued. "When I received your note mentioning blackmail, it all became clear. Les Gray was in your office to confront you with blackmail, not to check on Brian and me or whether Shawn Walker had children enrolled there."

"You're right," said Baksa. "Then he followed us to the Smoketown Elementary School to show me he meant business."

"Do you remember when I gave you Shawn Walker's photograph to examine here in the car?" asked Sammy. "The prints you left on that photograph matched the prints on the watch crystal. Then I knew for sure that you were Shawn Walker."

Mr. Baksa took the tin box. He sighed and recalled the day twenty-two years ago when he had placed this same box behind the stone. "When I ran away, I used the name Ray Miller, and rented a room from the Mellingers. I read the news item about my disappearance and decided to hide my watch. I didn't want to be Shawn Walker anymore."

Brian who was still recovering from the surprising disclosure leaned over from the back. "You really are Shawn Walker?"

The principal nodded. "I know you boys will keep this quiet."

"Why did you run away in the first place?" asked Brian.

"Oh, it was a combination of things. My dad expected me to be a doctor like himself. He pushed me into college to get a medical degree. I hated it. Then Les . . . I don't know why I ever considered him a friend. Now that I look back, I realize he was after my money. He'd tag along and I would buy him things. Then he'd borrow money from me and never pay it back."

"He's a con man, all right," said Brian.

"Then one day Les came to me and said that I was to say he was with me the previous

Wednesday afternoon. He said the police suspected him of robbing a grocery store."

"Did he?" asked Brian.

"Knowing Les, he probably did. He wanted me to be his alibi. When I refused, he got mad. He said if I didn't say he was with me at the time of the robbery, he'd tell the police I drove the getaway car."

"Wow," said Brian.

"That did it," said the principal. "I planned to disappear. I packed some clothes and took off. It may sound crazy now, but at the time, I just had to get away. My life was in a box. I was being controlled by others. I had no other way out, so I ran in order to be free."

"Your father withdrew twenty-five thousand dollars from the bank after you disappeared," said Sammy. "Do you know why?"

"I can guess. Les couldn't blackmail me because I disappeared. So he went to my dad. Probably told him I ran away because I helped him rob the store. And he would tell the police unless my father paid him the money."

"I'm curious," said Sammy. "What did Les Gray know about you that allowed him to find you so quickly?"

Mr. Baksa smiled. "He knew I always wanted to be a teacher. First thing he did when he arrived in Lancaster County was to visit the local colleges, Millersville and Franklin and Marshall. At Millersville he checked through the old yearbooks, starting with the late seventies. And there he saw my picture and recognized me. I had gone to the courthouse and changed my name to Michael Baksa."

"So Les Gray was able to use your new name and trace your teaching career," said Sammy.

"Yes, and he ended up at Conestoga Valley High School," said Baksa. "And that's when you saw him leave my office. He was there to blackmail me. He said that unless I paid him fifty thousand dollars, he would tell the Greensboro police where I was. He would also tell them that I helped him rob the store."

"Did you know he went to jail for that?" asked Brian.

"Yeah," he told me. "He blamed me. He was mad because I hadn't provided him with an alibi when he needed it."

Brian shook his head. "They always blame others for their mistakes."

"Was that your daughter who brought the note to my parents' shop?" asked Sammy.

"Yes, I told her the note had to do with a wall hanging I wanted to buy for the school. I had faith in you boys. I was hoping you could help me. And as it turned out you did. I want to thank you for that."

"Did you get your fifty thousand dollars back?" asked Sammy.

"Yeah, an old man came to the house with a duffel bag and said I should see that Shawn Walker gets it. I figured you boys had a hand in it."

"What about your money in the trust fund back in Greensboro?" asked Brian. "Did you know it was there? Are you going to get it?"

Sammy looked back at his friend. "That's none of our business, Brian."

"No, that's okay," said Mr. Baksa. "I was thinking about that back there when the sixth-grader asked the question. I didn't know of the money until I heard about it on the news. I knew my parents had money of course, but I didn't know about the trust fund. And since I don't want my father's money, at least for now, I'll keep the two million in the fund. But instead of the interest going to that Evans Investigations, I'll have it used for runaways, orphans, and disadvantaged children."

"That's great," said Sammy.

"Do you know what isn't so great?" asked Brian.

"What?" asked Sammy.

"Art Hansen won't have the full story in his book."

Sammy smiled. "That's what's going to make it a great book—guessing the truth about Shawn Walker."

"Some things are better left unsaid," said the principal. He took a deep breath and glanced at his watch. "We have to get back so you won't miss your bus." He started the car and headed for the high school.

Brian rested back against the seat and folded his arms across his chest. A large smile crossed his face. "You know what I just thought of, Sammy?"

"No, what?"

"I just thought of a way I can get all A's on my report card."

Laughter filled the car and didn't stop until the school buses came into view.

Michael Baksa is principal of the Conestoga Valley High School. His early life as portrayed in this story is fiction. I want to thank him for allowing me to tamper with his real world so Sammy and Brian would have a mystery to solve.

SAMMY AND BRIAN MYSTERY SERIES

#1 The Quilted Message by Ken Munro

The whole village was talking about it. Did the Amish quilt contain more than just twenty mysterious cloth pictures? The pressure was on for Bird-in-Hand's two teenage detectives, Sammy and Brian, to solve the mystery. Was Amos King murdered because of the quilt? Who broke into the country store? It was time for Sammy and Brian to unmask the intruder. $4.95

#2 Bird in the Hand by Ken Munro

When arson is suspected on an Amish farm, the village of Bird-in-Hand responds with a fund-raiser. The appearance of a mysterious tattooed man starts a series of events that ends in murder. And who is The Bird? Sammy and Brian are bound hand and foot by the feathered creature. Bird-in-Hand's own teenage sleuths break free and unravel the mystery. $5.95

#3 Amish Justice by Ken Munro

The duo turns into a trio when Joyce Myers becomes the newest member of the Sammy and Brian detective team. Is farmland in Lancaster County worth killing for? Frank Crawford thinks so. And when the police call the attempts on his life accidents, the old farmer sends for the teenage detectives. The three sleuths soon discover one of five suspects knows about the "IT" under the house. $5.95

#4 Jonathan's Journal by Ken Munro

After Scott Boyer comes to town, a young girl disappears. He then makes an offer Sammy and Brian can't refuse. A 200-year-old journal holds a challenge of a lifetime. It holds two secrets: a mysterious puzzle and murder. Bird-in-Hand's super detectives investigate the meaning behind its cryptic message. $5.95

#5 Doom Buggy by Ken Munro

An Amish buggy disappears. Twenty cut-out letters appear in its place. Then someone wants George Brock dead—in his welding shop. Sammy, Brian, and Joyce, fifteen-year-old sleuths from Bird-in-Hand, try to find the connection between these three mysterious happenings. $5.95

#6 **Fright Train** by Ken Munro
The actor, John Davenport, retires in Strasburg. He brings with him Manaus, the monster from his cult movie, *Fright Train.* While riding the Strasburg Railroad, Sammy and Brian learn that someone wants to steal something from the actor. But what? Is it his autobiography manuscript? Or is it the "Fright Train"? $5.95

#7 **Creep Frog** by Ken Munro
Where in Kitchen Kettle Village is Charles Parker? The frog isn't talking, but Zulu, the African parrot, has plenty to say. Charles Parker is masquerading under a new identity in Kitchen Kettle Village. U.S. Marshals want Sammy and Brian to find their hidden witness before Mack Roni, a thug, finds him. The frog is kidnapped, but why? And—will someone kiss the frog and turn him into Charles Parker? $5.95

#8 **The Number Game** by Ken Munro
Sidney Thomas, being chased by the police, has to make a hasty decision. Where can he hide a million dollars in diamonds at Root's Country Market? The mystery starts at the Conestoga Auction. Does the painting or the vase hold the secret to the diamonds? Joyce Myers joins Sammy and Brian in search of a briefcase full of diamonds. And—who is the masked man? $5.95

— —

These books may be purchased at your local bookstore or ordered from Gaslight Publishers, P. O. Box 258, Bird-in-Hand, PA 17505. Enclosed is $_____ (please add $2.00 for shipping and handling). Send check or money order only.

Name _____

Address _____

City_____ State_____ Zip Code _____